Raiders of Salt River Canyon

Craig Main

authorHOUSE®

AuthorHouse™
1663 Liberty Drive, Suite 200
Bloomington, IN 47403
www.authorhouse.com
Phone: 1-800-839-8640

First published by AuthorHouse 4/142009

ISBN: 978-1-4389-2125-9 (sc)

Printed in the United States of America
Bloomington, Indiana

This book is printed on acid-free paper.

This novel is dedicated to
Those who sacrifice their all to serve our country
As members of the United States Air Force,
Army, Navy, Marines and Coast Guard.

Thank you
For your service.

CAST OF CHARACTERS

Clint Wells, a former Texas Ranger, was a hardworking Arizona rancher devoted to the breeding of top-quality riding horses. But he was also a long-standing reserve member of the Arizona Rangers. And what appeared to be just another routine day for Clint at his Rim Shadow Ranch—with everything humming along perfectly—changed drastically the moment an unexpected visitor showed up on his doorstep.

Tom Williamson, the leader of a small group of Arizona Rangers stationed at Fort Verde, needed every man he could round up for a mission to Salt River Canyon. A band of ruthless raiders were robbing and killing innocent civilians north and south of the canyon. The latest victim was a rancher north of Globe. It was Williamson's job to stop them with every resource he had available to him.

Lisa Reavis Wells, the daughter of a Mexican sheep rancher and a redheaded Irish mother, was profoundly concerned when her husband, Clint, rode off to Salt River Canyon to assist the rangers. Little did she know that his dangerous mission would fall directly into her lap—with a horrifying conclusion.

Cal Amarē, the ruthless leader of a band of raiders, was fleeing for his life. He would do whatever it took to evade the rangers who were pursuing him—even if it meant killing an innocent woman and her child.

Chapter One

Before walking out of the kitchen, Clint gave the wall calendar a quick glance. It was Sunday, September 9, 1894.

Clint grabbed his hat from the coat "tree" as he headed out the front door to join his wife at the corral. He was instantly reminded of the change in seasons as he stepped onto the front porch. Fall was rapidly introducing itself to the Rim Shadow Ranch—bringing with it a perceptible chill in the air. The ranch was located at nearly six thousand feet above sea level; hence, the warmer days of summer were swiftly retreating. It seemed as though the mid-day sun was struggling more and more with each passing day to bathe the ranch with its warm rays.

Since its inception two years ago, Clint Wells' horse ranch has been an exceedingly busy place. Sales of his quality riding stock have grown far beyond his wildest dreams. His magnificent stallion, Liberty, has had a lot to do with the ranch's overwhelming success.

Like so many days before it, this day was moving along with scarcely any departure from the standard routine—that is, until a visitor arrived, unexpectedly, at the ranch.

Clint and Lisa were working near the corral when Tom Williamson rode in. It had been nearly three months since his last visit. Clint wondered: *Hmm, is this a social visit or is Tom here to seek my help, again?* Tom's prior visit had been purely a social call, but Clint was never sure what the leader of the local contingent of the Arizona Rangers had on his mind.

Six months ago, Williamson had stopped by to enlist Clint's help with tracking down a young outlaw that had held up Payson's only bank. They arrested the fugitive six days later without much ado. The amateur bank robber was now serving ten years in the territorial prison at Yuma—a harsh, unforgiving place where no man would ever wish to be incarcerated.

"Howdy, Tom!" greeted Clint, with a broad smile.

"Hello, Tom," echoed Lisa, with a slight hint of uneasiness in her voice.

"Hello, Clint … Lisa. How y'all been?"

"*Never better*, Tom," chirped Clint. "And you?"

"Doing quite well, Clint. Thanks for asking."

"Climb down from that tired ol' horse. We'll drift over to the house for a glass of Lisa's sweet apple cider."

"That sounds mighty good to me!"

Williamson dismounted and extended his hand to Clint. They readily shook hands. He tipped the brim of his hat to Lisa as he led his horse, Blanco, to the hitching rail.

"Tom, rest your bones in one of these ol' rockin' chairs," instructed Clint, when they arrived at the porch.

"Hey, I can handle that. I'm glad to see that they have soft seat cushions. That hard saddle was getting pretty rough on my aging tailbone," confessed Williamson, with a chuckle.

Reluctantly, Clint finally asked: "So, Tom, what brings ya out this way? Are ya on the trail of another outlaw?"

"Not just one … but a whole nest of 'em."

"What's going on, Tom?" asked Lisa, with trepidation.

"There's a large band of ruthless raiders working along the stagecoach route between Show Low and Globe … primarily in the Salt River Canyon region. I got a tip that they are holed up at the bottom of the canyon. I'm headin' for Show Low to have a chat with

Sheriff Ken Hannagan."

"Is Hannagan planning to assist you?" Clint asked.

"I doubt it, Clint. He's git'n up in years, and I don't think he could handle the strain. My sole objective is to get his permission to use his jail to incarcerate any prisoners that may get rounded up on this mission. I'm sure he—"

"Will you excuse me, gentlemen," interrupted Lisa, "while I go inside and fetch the cider?"

"By all means, Lisa," Clint responded.

"Certainly, ma'am. My throat is sure enough parched, and way overdue a nice cool drink," replied Williamson, while lightly stroking the front of his neck to stress his point.

"What were you about to say?" Clint asked.

"Uh … just that I'm certain Hannagan won't mind keepin' a few outlaws locked up in his jail for a short spell."

"So, Tom, where are the rest of your rangers? Are they waitin' for you in Show Low?"

"Jim O'Bryan and Will Clowers will be joining up with me there. You remember them, right?"

"Oh, yes … indeed! Where are they now?"

"Well, as of yesterday morning, they were at the train station in Flagstaff. They were scheduled to load their horses and gear aboard the eastbound train to Holbrook … and remain there overnight. If that went as planned … they should have rode out of Holbrook for Show Low this morning … arriving there sometime this evening."

"And where are your other men?" Clint inquired.

"Dave Martin and Geoff Tingle are presently in Prescott … and won't be able to join me. They've got a trial to attend. They're witnesses for the prosecution."

Frowning, Clint stated: "I very much hate to bring it up … but it looks like you are a bit skeletal on help."

"Yes, that I am! And *that*, my friend, is what brought me to your door … to request *your* capable support."

At that very moment, Lisa stepped out onto the porch with two tall glasses of cider. "I was afraid of that," quipped Lisa, not looking too happy.

Lisa surrendered the drinks to Williamson and Clint. Both men smiled and thanked her. She then quickly backed away a few paces and braced herself for what was to come.

With a sincere look of apology on his face, Ranger Williamson guardedly made his plea to Lisa, saying: "I'm very sorry, ma'am, but I *really* need you husband's professional assistance for the next several days."

"Tom, you know I always support the rangers," Lisa said, as she stared forlornly across the courtyard. Then she finally asked: "So, Tom, when do you plan to cart him off?"

"Well, I'm hoping I can borrow a bed in your bunkhouse for the night, and then we'll ride out in the morning."

"In the morning!" exclaimed Lisa, with a deep sigh.

Clint looked at Lisa. He could clearly see that she was not pleased with his leaving on such short notice.

"Lisa, I—I am so sorry. I do hope you'll be okay with this," Clint finally managed to say.

"Yes, I'm *okay* with it … but I don't have to like it." She moved closer to her husband, bent over, and hugged his neck. "It's just that I worry so when you are away."

"I know. I'll be extra careful for you and Lena. Can't have my baby daughter growin' up without her daddy."

"Then it's settled, Clint?" asked Williamson, not quite sure yet of his answer.

"Yes, Tom. How much stuff do I need to pack?"

"Just a change of clothes. Will and Jim will purchase all our necessary provisions tomorrow at the mercantile store in Show Low. They will also purchase some packhorses from the local livery.

"You and I will spend Monday night in Show Low, and leave out at first light Tuesday morning for the canyon."

Clint nodded, then said: "Fine. Now, Tom, take care of your horse … then come to the house for some lunch."

As Williamson untied Blanco from the hitching rail, he could not help but notice how tired his horse looked. He patted Blanco's sweaty neck and said aloud: "Don't worry, my friend, we aren't going anywhere. It's time to get you unsaddled, groomed, watered and fed. We're gonna stay the night."

Clint thought it wise to join Lisa in the kitchen. He wanted to give her the opportunity to fully respond, in private, to his upcoming departure.

"Lisa, are you *sure* you're okay with my being away?" he asked, while looking directly into her green eyes. He knew her eyes disclosed more than any of her verbal responses.

"Yes, Clint. Lena and I will be fine. Please let our neighbors know that you're leaving with Tom. I'm sure they won't mind checking in on us each day that you are away."

"I can do that," Clint said. Then he rambled on in an effort to ease Lisa's doubts and fears, saying: "And thankfully, you'll not be *all* alone. It's good that Jenny and her children are still living with us. Maree and Kris have become a big help to us over the past couple years. They sure have grown up."

Lisa, too, was glad that her brother's wife and children had come to live with them after his untimely death. Ramon, intoxicated at the time, had picked a fight with two hardcore cowboys and died from a severe knife wound inflicted by one of them. Both fled the countryside, and have not been seen since. Payson's town marshal, Mike Chandler, long ago, distributed wanted posters for both men. A reward was set at *one thousand dollars* each for Ty Roper and Forrest Woods.

"Hold me, Clint," begged Lisa, while reaching for him.

Clint put his arms around his wife and held her for the longest time. Soon their lips met. Their love for each other had grown stronger and stronger over the past two years. They were a team, and as such, shared equally in everything that touched their lives. God had certainly blessed their union.

While stroking Lisa's long red hair, Clint said: "Reckon we'd best get Tom's lunch ready before he returns."

She wanted to remain in Clint's embrace a good deal longer but knew that wasn't possible at the moment. She realized she would be in his arms tonight, and that she would hold him all night long—if that's what it took to erase her fears.

* * * * *

Next door, at the Double Creek Ranch, Robert Lynne was busy at the corral saddling up his mare, Star, for a ride to Clint's ranch.

His wife, Rebecca, was sitting on the porch chatting with his sister, Connie. Shortly after Robert and Rebecca married, Connie moved out of her brother's home, and built her own home just forty yards north of Robert's barn—along the lane leading to the main road.

And not long after the house was finished, Connie's beloved aunt, Helen Myers, sold her Corydon, Indiana, home and came west to live with her. For Connie's departure from Corydon in 1892 left Mrs. Myers without any living family members in Indiana.

"Robert!" shouted Connie.

No response.

"Robert!"

Robert turned about and saw his sister waving her hand in the air. Having finished with the saddling of Star, he walked to the porch with his mare in-tow.

"What's up, Sis?"

"Are you headed over to Clint's place?"

"Sure am. Have you a request?"

"Yes, brother. Be a dear, and invite Clint and Lisa over for dinner tomorrow evening. And Lena, too!"

"Can do, Sis! See y'all in a little while."

Robert filled his saddle, and rode at a fast trot down the lane toward the main road. Now, Clint's ranch house was just three hundred yards due west (through the dense pine forest) from Robert's house, and in truth, Robert could have walked there using a well-worn path that had its starting point behind the bunkhouse, but he wanted to give Star some exercise.

* * * * *

A light knock at the front door announced that Ranger Williamson had returned to the house for lunch.

"Come on in, Tom!" shouted Clint, from the kitchen.

Williamson pulled open the screen door, entered the house, and propped his new carbine against the wall by the door. Spotting the coat "tree," he removed his hat and hung it on one of the protruding wooden pegs.

"Please, have a seat at the table," instructed Clint.

"Tom, do you need to wash up first?" Lisa asked.

"Why, yes, I do. Thank you."

Lisa grabbed a porcelain-lined pan and walked over to the water pump. "I'll fetch some fresh water for you."

Lisa filled the pan with water and motioned to her guest that it was ready for his use. She placed a clean towel and a bar of soap near the pan.

Williamson hastily washed up, and joined Lisa and Clint at the table. As they were preparing to say the blessing, a horse could be heard approaching the house.

Rising quickly from the kitchen table, Clint walked to the front screen door to have a look outside.

"Who is it, Clint?" Lisa inquired.

Smiling, Clint replied: "It's our neighbor, Robert."

Clint went out onto the porch to greet his best friend and business partner. "Say, my friend, what brings you by?"

Remaining in the saddle, Robert responded, saying: "I'm sending Charlie to Payson tomorrow to buy supplies … and I thought I'd come over and see if y'all needed anything."

"That's mighty thoughtful of ya, Rob. Abandon that saddle and come on in the house. I'd like for you to have lunch with us … and greet an ol' friend of ours. Have you the time?"

"Certainly, Clint. Who is it?"

Smiling again, Clint said: "You'll see."

As soon as Robert entered the house and glanced across the room, he saw Williamson.

"Well, I'll be doggone!" exclaimed Robert. "Now just how long has it been since I last laid eyes on you? Maybe three months … maybe longer?"

"At *least* that," confirmed Williamson, while standing to shake Robert's extended hand.

"What brings ya to these parts? Can't be to catch outlaws … cause you and Clint ran them all off two years ago during your big campaign atop the Mogollon Rim."

"Well, yes, that was quite an undertaking. Thankfully, we haven't had any more trouble at the Mogollon Rim Ranch since Wes Baden and his cutthroat riders were either killed or locked up," voiced Tom, with an air of satisfaction.

Robert continued to quiz the ranger. "Just passin' through then?" he asked.

"Hardly!" snapped Lisa, still showing her displeasure.

"Oh—oh, I think I smell trouble," surmised Robert, while glancing from Lisa back to Clint.

"This time ... Tom has come on business. He's asked me to join up with him ... to deal with a serious problem over near Globe," explained Clint.

"I see. And you'll be riding out soon?" Robert asked.

"Yes, early in the morning. And I'd like for you to check on my family while I'm gone ... if you don't mind."

"Hey, Clint, you know I don't mind one bit."

"Thanks, Rob. That takes a lot of worry off of me."

"Oh, before I forget ... Connie would like for you and Lisa to come by for dinner tomorrow evening. But now it looks as though that *won't* be happening."

"Excuse me, Robert, but it certainly *will* happen!" corrected Lisa. "Tell Connie I would love to come by. Have you a time in mind?"

"Oh, five o'clock would be fine." Then he added: "And be sure to bring Lena."

"I wouldn't *dream* of leaving her behind."

"Say, where is Lena, anyway?" Robert asked.

"She's out back playing with Maree and Kris. Jenny is watching her," Lisa answered.

Everyone continued to chitchat during lunch. Most of the conversation generated by the men centered around an event that happened over two years ago—during the spring of 1892—when Clint, Williamson, and six other rangers rode against the outlaws at Wes Baden's Mogollon Rim Ranch. Eighteen men (including Baden) and one woman died during that two-day campaign. Sadly, two of the dead were rangers Bud Wilcox and Chuck Carson.

Of all the dead outlaws, the most feared was the Tonto Basin Kid. His real name was Billy Blackheart. During his lifetime—which was short in years—he had maliciously killed a total of eleven men. He refused to be taken in alive, and was killed in a hail of gunfire.

Another of the dead outlaws was Frank Carver, a fugitive from Texas. He had come to Arizona with the sole purpose of killing Clint Wells.

During his days as a Texas Ranger, Clint hunted down and arrested Frank's brother, Wayne, on a charge of murder. Wayne was later hanged. The man that Wayne killed was Clint's brother, Chad. Chad was a peace officer in San Angelo who, at the time, had tried to stop Wayne from robbing a bank—and was killed for his effort.

Frank Carver died in a face-to-face gun battle with Clint at the Baden ranch. Clint had received a serious head wound as a result. The two men were just about equally matched when it came to squaring off in a showdown. Clint won out by a mere split-second over Carver.

"Say, Clint, does your head still ache where Carver's bullet tore a groove in it?" inquired Williamson.

"Eh, sometimes, but not all that much," answered Clint, while rubbing the scar just above his left temple.

"I thought for sure you were dead when I seen ya sprawled there on the ground. I'm glad it was Carver and not you that got buried under three feet of soil that day," sighed Williamson, while shaking his head.

"Ya got that right, Tom," Clint quickly agreed. "If he'd been just a hair quicker it would have been me up there on the Rim inhaling that mound of dirt."

"Clint, please, stop such talk," begged Lisa, somewhat teary eyed. "I just don't think I can bear to hear anymore dreadful talk about killing and dying."

"Oh, by all means. I'm very sorry, Lisa," replied Clint, apologetically. "Not another word."

Williamson and Robert Lynne apologized as well.

Robert scooted his chair back from the table and stood up. "Clint, I must get back to my ranch. I'll get Dusty Rhodes to help me with the stage duties while you're gone. You just be real careful this week … and come back to us in one piece."

"Rob, I'm glad you came by," replied Clint, smiling.

"Ranger Williamson, it's good to see you again. Don't be such a stranger," Robert said, extending his hand.

"Good to see you again, Robert," replied Williamson, while shaking Robert's hand.

While waving his hand, Robert said: "*Adios*, Lisa. I'll let Connie know that you *will* be by tomorrow evening."

"*¡Hasta mañana!*" affirmed Lisa, in a sprightly tone.

Clint Wells and Ranger Williamson followed Robert Lynne out onto the porch, and watched as he mounted up and rode off down the lane.

"Well, Tom, I'd like to know more about this deal you are dragging me into. Let's sit a spell here on the porch and you can fill me in on the details."

For the next twenty minutes, Williamson explained as much about the job as was possible. It would not be an easy campaign. Most weren't. And, personnel wise, they would be short-handed. They both realized that without veterans like Dave Martin and Geoff Tingle to watch their backs, it would make the mission much more dangerous.

"Any chance we'll get some help from the United States marshal?" asked Clint, hoping for a miracle.

"No chance of that. But, I do have a new man that is supposed to meet us south of Show Low on Tuesday. He hasn't been a ranger very long, but his supervisor highly recommended him. That's all the extra help we're going to get."

"What's his name?"

"Jess McCain. He's been a ranger about ten months. A young fella, maybe twenty-one … or there 'bouts."

"I hope we don't have to baby-sit him."

"Reckon we'll find out soon enough, Clint."

"Say, Tom, I've been meaning to ask ya something for the past hour. What's with that shinny new insignia on your shirt collar?"

"Oh, that. Well, Clint, I've been promoted to captain. It came with a small pay raise too."

"Well, if that ain't dandy then I don't know what is! Congratulations, Tom—uh—I mean Captain!"

"Thanks, Clint. I hope I do the new position proud. Maybe one day I'll get promoted to the district office in Flagstaff … and sit at a comfy desk for a change."

"That would certainly beat being shot at by a bunch of low-down, cantankerous outlaws!"

With a broad smile forming on his aging face, Williamson heartily replied, saying: "You won't get an argument from me!"

Several minutes later, Lisa joined them on the porch. The conversation quickly changed to something more pleasant. Neither man had any desire to upset her again.

* * * * *

Robert did not return to his ranch right away. He took Star on a five-mile journey up and down the main road to give her some much-needed exercise. He had not ridden her in four or five days.

Star was one of finest Quarter Horse mares that Robert ever had the pleasure of owning. She had even been a part of Clint's horse breeding efforts. Last year, she produced a fine little filly. Rebecca named her Lilly. She would, one day, belong to their first-born child.

Clint had promised to train the new mare for Robert. Most folks around the Mogollon Rim often commented that Clint was one of those *horse whisper* types. They based their opinion on the natural way he went about getting the best out of all his horses.

Robert completed his ride, unsaddled Star, and rubbed her down before allowing her to drink any water. After putting her back in her stall, he returned to the house to inform his sister, Connie, that Lisa and Lena would be coming by for supper on Monday at five o'clock—but not Clint.

Connie was markedly upset and vocal when she learned *why* Clint would not be joining them.

"Why can't they just leave the man alone? He has a family now … and the other rangers don't. He doesn't need to be chasing after another gang of hardcore killers."

Robert was unsure just how to reply to her reasonable argument. He took in a deep breath, then replied, saying: "Sis, I don't know why. But it might have a lot to do with his invaluable experience as a lawman, *and* because he can always be depended on to do the right thing when the action heats up."

"Well, it just doesn't seem fair," complained Connie, her anger lessening somewhat.

"Sis, if I didn't know better, I'd think you were harboring some special feelings for the man."

Connie didn't defend herself against his indictment. She walked away instead. Her brother had hit a nerve—one that she didn't know still existed.

Two years ago, during the spring of 1892, there had been some minor history between Clint and Connie. Clint could not make up his mind which woman he loved most—Lisa or Connie; and Connie could not decide which man she loved most—Clint or Pastor Rick Vargas.

Clint met Lisa Reavis during his initial visit to Payson. He was there to search for some ranch land, she to visit her brother. Her wonderfully spirited personality captivated him. They fell in love almost immediately. Four days later, Lisa returned to her home in Springerville; and Clint, not finding any suitable land near Payson, returned to the Double Creek Ranch to enter into a business partnership with Robert Lynne. It was then and there that he met Connie. She had recently arrived from Indiana to live with her brother. Clint was instantly bowled over by her beauty and demeanor. Thoughts of Lisa, for a brief period of time, took a back seat to Connie.

Connie met Pastor Vargas while en route from Indiana to Robert's ranch. They were on the same stagecoach during the last leg of her journey. He didn't show much interest in her at the time, but two months later (after corresponding often by mail) he began to court her on a fairly steady basis.

By mid-summer, Clint was the first to reveal his feelings. He decided that his heart belonged to Lisa. Connie was highly disappointed by his decision, but in due time she accepted it. In fact, she even went so far as to convince herself that her love for Clint had been nothing more than what a sister might feel for a brother. From that point on, she focused her full attention on Pastor Vargas. Several months later she announced her engagement to the pastor.

Clint—as soon as construction of his ranch house was completed—asked Lisa for her hand in marriage. They were married two weeks later. Pastor Vargas even performed the ceremony. Just nine days ago, on September 1, Clint and Lisa celebrated their second anniversary.

Chapter Two

As the waning sunlight changed ever so quickly into darkness, Clint and Lisa got little thirteen-month-old Lena off to bed, and then themselves. Before retiring, Clint had gotten his bedroll, clothes, and other personal items laid out for his early morning trip with Captain Williamson. He had also spent part of the afternoon making sure Liberty was ready to ride. The stallion's shoes and hooves were carefully checked; and he was given extra feed. Clint even checked over his tack to be sure it was in good repair.

As they were lying in bed, Lisa snuggled up close to Clint. She put her arm across his chest and rested her head on his shoulder.

"My darling husband, I do wish you were not putting yourself in danger again," sighed Lisa.

"It will be okay, my *little mountain girl*. Just keep me in your daily prayers. We must always trust in our Heavenly Father to take care of us … no matter what comes our way. Nothing will happen to me but what He allows. I never ride out in fear, for I know that He is ever watching over me," professed Clint, hoping to reassure his wife.

"Yes, you're right. I *will* pray for you every day … just as I do when you are here with me," she confessed.

"You do? I'm so happy to hear that."

"Please, hold me, Clint, like you've never held me before … if that's possible."

Clint took her in his arms, and cradled her for the longest time. Eventually, he sought her lips and began to kiss her passionately. He could feel Lisa rapidly responding to his lovemaking. She pulled him even tighter against her slender body, and returned kiss for kiss, each one increasing in its intensity. In short order, both were burning with voracious desire for the other.

Clint turned aside the thin blanket that covered him and Lisa. He eagerly blazed a trail filled with kisses that extended from her lips, down her neck, and ended at her breast—which were now heaving with excitement. She gladly yielded to his every kiss and gentle caress.

Clint left little of her radiant anatomy unexplored. After several minutes of indescribable pleasure, Lisa motioned for her husband to return his lips to hers. As Clint repositioned himself, she spread her wings and invited him to partake of all she had to offer. For the next couple of hours, the entire world and all its problems were tuned out. There was only the two of them—and that was all that mattered at the moment.

Clint and Lisa were fully aware that there was no promise of a tomorrow. Both were determined to live out each day to its fullest. The love between Clint and Lisa could not be stronger. And, more importantly, they had a loving respect for each other that went beyond any known measure.

* * * * *

Six o'clock arrived much too early for Clint. He stumbled out of bed. However, it only took him thirty minutes to wash, dress, and eat breakfast. (Lisa had his breakfast waiting for him by the time he got to the kitchen.)

When he went outside, he spotted Williamson at the corral saddling his big, white gelding, Blanco. This was the horse once ridden by Frank Carver—the man who tried to kill Clint. Williamson took possession of the horse following Carver's death. *To the victor goes all the good stuff,* was Williamson's comment that day at the Mogollon Rim Ranch.

Clint couldn't very well fault Williamson for taking a horse, because he, too, claimed a dead man's horse that day—a piebald pony belonging to none other than the Tonto Basin Kid. The pony, Cholla, was now the favorite mount of Jenny's two children.

"Good morning, Tom!" Clint said, still feeling a bit sleepy. He was also feeling very tired from all his and Lisa's lovemaking during the night. But that wasn't something to be shared with his friend.

"Good morning to you, Clint!"

"Looks like it's time to go, huh?" sighed Clint, while secretly wishing that he could delay his departure.

"Yeah. I reckon we need to get moving if we want to reach Show Low before sunset."

Clint retrieved Liberty from his stall; and began the planned process of getting his mount ready to travel. In a few short minutes, Liberty was ready to ride. His big, liver-colored stallion appeared to be excited about the upcoming journey.

Clint carefully inspected his carbine, and slipped it into the scabbard. Next, he checked his Colt, and holstered it. He looped the small piece of leather over the hammer to prevent the Colt from popping out of the holster while he was riding.

Before mounting up, Clint walked back to the house to say his final farewell to his wife and daughter. He walked into Lena's bedroom and found her fast asleep. He leaned over the bed rail and gave her a kiss on the forehead. She was the second greatest joy of his life. He would greatly miss her.

Clint held his greatest joy, Lisa, in his arms for a long moment. No one spoke right away. Then he gave her a final kiss, and reluctantly released his hold on her.

"I love you," she gladly confessed.

Suddenly she thought back to the time when she first realized she loved this fearless and adventurous man. She had not been able to confess her love for him then. Had it been fear of rejection? She didn't know. Whatever it was then, it certainly seemed foolish to her now.

"I love you more," he said, grinning.

"That's not possible, and you know it," she shot back, while feeling her heart skip a beat at his revelation to her.

"I'll return to you, my love, as quickly as I can. Keep the rangers in your prayers too."

Clint softly stroked Lisa's cheek, did an about-face, and departed for the corral. He was soon mounted and turning Liberty's head toward the lane. Before disappearing from Lisa's sight, he turned in the saddle and gave her one last wave.

* * * * *

On Saturday, Will Clowers and Jim O'Bryan left Flagstaff, as scheduled, on the eastbound Santa Fe train for Holbrook. They arrived mid-afternoon.

On Sunday, they traveled south—on horseback—to Show Low. They arrived in Show Low a couple of hours before sunset. Show Low was where they planned to rendezvous with their boss, Captain Williamson.

It was now Monday morning, and both men were feeling the soreness from yesterday's long ride. Today they would go to the local mercantile store and gather up the supplies that they would need for their trip to the Salt River Canyon.

"Do you think the boss was able to talk our pal, Wells, into comin' along on this new deal?" Jim asked.

"Not sure," Will replied. He paused a moment, then added, saying: "We can only hope."

"Yeah. He's a good man, and we certainly need his expertise," said Jim, with a somber look on his face.

"I wouldn't worry none. Wells won't let us down. He's too good a friend for that," responded Will, confidently.

"Let's get some grub in our bellies, and then make a beeline for the mercantile store. We've got a lot to do today before the boss arrives," Jim declared.

"I'm ready when you are!"

* * * * *

Around mid-day, Clint Wells and Captain Williamson stopped to rest; and partake of the sack lunches that Lisa had thoughtfully prepared for them.

"Say, Tom, did I ever tell you what Robert's sister, Connie, is planning to do?"

"Not sure, Clint. What would that be?"

"Well, Connie, with major financial backing from her aunt, is planning to open a mercantile store along the stagecoach route … near Christopher Creek. She seems to think that that area is prime for development."

"Ya don't say," replied Williamson, with interest.

"I think she's on to somethin' big. It sure would be nice if folks livin' in the area didn't have to drive a wagon all the way to Payson or Show Low to purchase supplies. A store in that location would certainly be close to my ranch.

"And that's not all … she plans to add a café next to her store. A café would be a welcomed stop for stage travelers. Hey, they gotta eat like everyone else."

"That sounds like an innovative plan. Is she going to get started on it any time soon?" asked Williamson, his interest growing by leaps and bounds.

"Robert says it's already movin' forward. The land has been purchased, the survey is completed, and the materials have been ordered for the building."

"When does she expect to open her store?"

"Next spring, I believe she said. Connie is already signing up some local carpenters to erect the building. I think Charlie Rhodes is gonna supervise the project. He's quite the carpenter, you know."

"I wonder what other businesses could benefit in that location?" asked Williamson, while stroking his chin.

"What about a hotel, or a livery, or maybe a blacksmith shop?" Clint quickly suggested—off the top of his head.

"Yeah. They all sound pretty good to me!"

Both men finished their lunches, and mounted up. Soon they were back on the road to Show Low.

As they were riding along, Clint's mind was running in circles trying to think of other ways to make money to support his ranch.

Then it suddenly hit him: *A dude ranch!*

Eastern visitors to the Mogollon Rim were always looking for ways to experience the Wild West. What a great way to satisfy their yearning. Clint exclaimed inwardly to himself: *A dude ranch it will be!*

Clint was about to share his idea with Williamson, but promptly changed his mind. Perhaps he would later—much later. However, he would definitely share his idea with Robert as soon as he got home.

Over the next several miles, Clint quietly pondered what all it would take to support a dude ranch for those "adventure-starved" Easterners. They would need lodging, meals, and scheduled activities to keep them busy.

Clint felt certain that he was overlooking many of the necessary requirements, but when he returned home, he would sit down with Robert, Rebecca and Lisa, and sort out all the various details.

"You've been mighty quite the past few miles, Clint. Is everything okay?"

"Oh, indeed it is, Tom. I was just thinking about all the possibilities that some sort of new business could provide to the Mogollon Rim region."

* * * * *

It was getting late in the afternoon by the time Will and Jim finished up their shopping spree at the mercantile store. The owner, Howard Simmons, and his nephew, Jimmy, had been very helpful. Jimmy had even helped the rangers load their supplies onto the packhorses.

As they were finishing up, Jimmy asked: "Where ya rangers headin' with all this stuff?"

Jim quickly explained that they were meeting up with some other rangers and traveling to the Salt River Canyon to round up some raiders that had been robbing the stagecoach and terrorizing law-abiding citizens.

"They killed a man over near Globe," added Will.

"A ranger's job is never done," Jim concluded.

"My uncle met a *Texas* Ranger once, but it was a couple of years back," Jimmy proudly announced.

When Will Clowers hastily countered that he knew a Texas Ranger, too—by the name of Clint Wells—Jimmy's jaw dropped to his chest. His faced beamed.

"I've heard o' him!" exclaimed Jimmy. "He's the same ranger my Uncle Howard met."

With that knowledge, Will re-entered the mercantile store, and said: "Mister Simmons! Sorry to bother you, sir, but I was just outside talking to Jimmy … and he says you know a ranger by the name of Clint Wells."

"Why, yes, I do! He was in my store two years ago. Last I heard … he was being pursued by an outlaw … a man named Carver, I believe."

"Yep, that would shore be the one. Well, sir, ya might be interested in knowin' that Ranger Wells is now workin' with the *Arizona* Rangers, and may be arriving in Show Low this very afternoon."

"Oh, that's splendid! Please ask him to stop by my store when he arrives. I would very much like to talk with him. I owe the man an apology."

"You do? What ever for?" Will inquired.

Mr. Simmons dropped his head. "Well, it's sort of a personal matter. Ranger Wells can tell you about it if he so chooses. Anyway, please, ask him to stop by my store."

"I'll certainly let him know that you want to see him," promised Will, as he left the store and rejoined his partner—and Jimmy.

"You were right, Jimmy," Will began, "he did know our ranger friend. And, he wants to see him when he arrives in town today."

"That's grand!" Jimmy cried. "I want to meet him too."

* * * * *

It was nearly five o'clock when Clint Wells and Captain Williamson rode into Show Low. Both were dog-tired.

"Clint, let's drop by the livery stable and deposit these horses. After that, we'll secure a room at the hotel."

"And don't forget … we need to nail down a hot meal, too," proclaimed Clint, while patting his growling stomach.

"Yes, Clint, by all means. But before we fill our bellies, we must pay Sheriff Hannagan a visit … *and* … see if we can locate Will and Jim."

With the horses being cared for at the livery, the two rangers walked to the nearest hotel. The desk clerk greeted them cordially as they approached the long wooden counter, saying: "Afternoon, gentlemen. And welcome to the Whispering Pines Hotel. Please sign the register."

After both rangers had signed the page, the clerk spun the register around and looked at the names. "Oh, yes, I've been expecting you." Then he handed a room key to Williamson and a folded sheet of paper to Clint.

"It's a message from those other two rangers that stayed here last night. Not certain why they checked out this morning," concluded the clerk.

"I'm guessing that they are probably bivouacking tonight somewhere near town," Williamson replied to the clerk.

Clint unfolded the note and began reading aloud:

> *Captain. Got all the supplies rounded up. We will camp one mile south of town on the road to Globe. Do not want to leave the supplies unattended. Stop by as soon as you can. P.S. If Clint is with you, tell him to stop at the mercantile store. The owner wants to speak with him. Jim.*

Clint scratched at the side of his face, and said: "Hmm, I wonder what that could be about?"

"Better go and see," suggested Williamson. "I'll check out our room … and meet you over there in a few minutes."

Clint departed the hotel, and made a beeline for the one and only mercantile store. He knew the place well, as he had shopped there—buying supplies and getting directions—over two years ago. In a couple of minutes he was pushing back the door to enter.

"Ranger Wells!" exclaimed Mr. Simmons. "It's such a pleasure to see you again. You have no idea how many times I have thought about you."

Clint and the store's owner chatted politely for several minutes. Before concluding their conversation, Mr. Simmons presented Clint with an apology. Clint was immediately taken aback. He told the merchant that his apology was completely unnecessary. But Mr. Simmons insisted on offering it anyway.

"Mister Simmons, you did nothing wrong."

"Yes, I did. I should never have given that outlaw information about you. My mistake nearly got you killed."

"Sir, Frank Carver would have found me, with or without your help. He's quite dead … and I'm still alive. It really doesn't matter anymore."

"And you don't know how grateful I am that you are alive," sighed the merchant. "Praise God for that."

At that moment, Captain Williamson entered the store. Clint gladly introduced him to Mr. Simmons. The three of them chatted briefly, and then parted company. It had seemed strange to Clint that the elderly merchant had felt so responsible for his welfare.

"What was that all about, Clint?"

"Not sure, Tom. Somehow or another, Simmons felt responsible for Frank Carver and me meeting up. He said he thought Carver was a good friend of mine when he told him where to find me."

"He did? That wasn't too smart."

"Tom, I believe Carver would have found me even if precautions had been taken. A man full of revenge doesn't give up too easily."

"I can't very well argue with that. Now, my friend, let's go chat a spell with Sheriff Hannagan. After that, we'll go searching for two big, juicy steaks. Do ya know of a good place to eat in this town?"

"Sure do, Tom … the Blue Moon Café!"

* * * * *

Ninety minutes later, Clint and his boss arrived at the campsite south of town. Neither Jim nor Will seemed all that surprised to see Clint. Greetings were immediately exchanged.

After some small talk, Williamson changed the subject matter to items that were much more serious in nature.

"Men, we are gonna have our work cut out for us on this mission. We are shorthanded for starters. Thankfully, we have a man joining up with us en route."

"How many raiders do you think we are up against, Captain?" Jim asked.

"Not really sure. Perhaps as many as a dozen."

"What can ya tell us about this here canyon?" inquired Will. "I ain't never in my life been down that way."

"Well, I asked Sheriff Hannagan about it. He says it's deep … maybe as much as two thousand feet from the rim to the river below. Also, the road is treacherous … narrow and full of hairpin curves. If ya get too close to the edge … you're likely to fall to your death. From the rim above … it's over four miles by roadway to the river below."

"It sounds to me like this canyon is *more* dangerous than the raiders we're after!" exclaimed Jim, with a big sigh. "I fear we could die just trying to get down into that canyon."

"That's a real possibility, Jim," replied Williamson, with a shake of his head. "Hannagan says the canyon has a nickname: The *little* Grand Canyon!"

"Well, it don't sound so little to me," Clint countered.

Soon, plans were outlined for the next day. Everyone agreed to meet at the campsite at seven o'clock in the morning.

Clint and Captain Williamson returned to Show Low, and to their hotel room. It had been a long day in the saddle, and both were worn out. A good night's sleep was what they needed most. The new day would arrive way too soon.

* * * * *

It was nearly dark by the time Lisa and Lena returned home. They had enjoyed a great meal at the home of Connie Lynne and Helen Myers.

Much of the conversation during dinner had centered on the plans for the new mercantile store and café that would be coming soon to Christopher Creek. Lisa was very happy for them, and wished them the greatest success. She was aware that neither woman had had any source of income since coming to Arizona, and that both women were anxious to improve their financial circumstances.

Mrs. Myers had nearly three thousand dollars remaining from

the sale of her property in Corydon, Indiana, but it wouldn't last indefinitely. And Connie had received a *gift* of nearly eighteen hundred dollars from Sheriff Hannagan two years ago, after he killed Reed Dagon—the man that had attempted to rape and kill her. (The lawman found the money in Dagon's pocket, and gave it to Connie for all her pain and suffering at the hands of the despicable gambler.) But that money had been used to build her new house. In truth, Connie was virtually broke. Her generous aunt was providing the money required for the mercantile store and café.

Lisa was glad to have such wonderful and kind neighbors living so close at hand. Each was always there for the other in time of need.

Lisa put Lena to bed. And before retiring, she spent some time chatting with Jenny.

"Where are Maree and Kris?" Lisa asked.

"They've already gone to bed. Both were very tired," Jenny answered.

"Looks like it will just be us around here for the next several days. I just hate it that Clint has gone off hunting outlaws again," sighed Lisa.

"Don't worry, *mi cuñada*! He will return to us. We must pray for him and the others."

"You can count on me doing that," Lisa vowed.

"Lisa, may I ask you something … something very, very personal?"

"Certainly. What is it? You sound so serious."

"What do you think of Dusty Rhodes?"

"I think he is a fine, upstanding, young man. Why do you ask?"

"I'm hopelessly in love with him. I know he's much younger than me … but it doesn't seem to matter to him."

"Yes, he's only twenty-one. Does he love you?"

"Yes, he has told me so … many times. And he loves the children too."

"What do the children think about him?"

"They are crazy about him. He really relates to them. And they sorely need a father. Maree is already fourteen, and Kris just turned twelve. I don't want them to be without a man in their life … to show them how to survive in this world."

"You are only eight years older than Dusty … so I don't see a problem. Just look at how much older Clint is than me. We don't have any problems with age. I wouldn't worry so much about it. Go with your heart, Jenny."

"Thank you, Lisa. I shall do just that."

Lisa and Jenny talked on and on for at least another hour. Lisa was pleased about that. She hated crawling into an empty bed. There was nothing she enjoyed more at night than cuddling up to the man she dearly loved. It meant more to her than life itself.

She wondered where her adventurous man was at the moment, and if he was doing all right. She knelt beside her bed and lifted up her prayer to God, and asked Him to watch over the man she loved.

With that done, she lay down on the bed and pulled the thin blanket over her body. She turned her head and looked at the unused pillow next to her. She suddenly felt very lonely.

Chapter Three

Tuesday morning brought with it a noticeable chill in the air. The leaves were already beginning to display their fall colors. Show Low, which rested at an elevation above six thousand feet, typically experienced an early onset of winter.

It was approaching seven o'clock when Clint Wells and Captain Tom Williamson arrived at the campsite established by Jim O'Bryan and Will Clowers. After breaking camp, the four rangers lit out on a fifty-two-mile journey to Salt River Canyon—a taxing trek that could take nine to ten hours.

"Gentlemen, I don't know if we can reach the canyon before sunset or not. To rush headlong down there could put a lot of stress on our horses *and* us. If we put at least *forty* miles under our saddles today … then by golly … I think we will have done very well," Williamson reasoned.

"Ya won't get no argument from me, Captain," Will quickly proclaimed.

"That goes for me too!" Jim chimed in.

"That's good. We'll rest our horses about every hour or so. This is rough country out here, and a man without a horse is as good as dead," instructed Williamson, with a word of caution thrown in for good measure.

It was almost nine o'clock when the four rangers reined up in front of the Juniper Woods way station. This station, as with all the others along this route, was owned and operated by the Canyon Stage Company.

"How far have we come, Captain?" Jim asked. "My tailbone is git'n rather numb!"

"Maybe sixteen miles," Williamson guessed. "We'll take a longer break here and water the horses."

"And just where are we meetin' up with this other ranger," Will inquired.

"Carrizo Creek," Williamson answered. "He's riding over from Fort Apache … a distance of about twenty-six miles. He should have left there early this morning."

"He might already be sit'n there … just waitin' fer us to show up," suggested Jim.

"He very well could be," Williamson agreed.

As soon as the horses were watered, the command to depart was issued. "Break is over, men, let's ride!" ordered Williamson, as he swung his leg over the cantle of his saddle.

* * * * *

Lisa Wells and Rebecca Lynne were having lunch together at the Basin Flat two-room schoolhouse where they both were employed as teachers. Rebecca could tell that Lisa was not her usual happy self, and decided to inquire about her state.

"It's Clint, right? I know you are worried, Lisa, but everything will be okay. Your man will be home soon."

Lisa's shoulders were slumped over. "Yes, it's Clint. I just don't know what I would do if I lost him to some outlaw's skill with a gun. It would probably be the death of me."

"Be strong … *little mountain girl*!"

Lisa corrected her posture. "What did you call me?"

"Isn't that what Clint calls you?"

"How did *you* know that?" asked Lisa, with a puzzled look on her pretty face. "That's supposed to be Clint's *secret* pet name for me."

"Oh, I've got good ears. I heard him teasing you the other day … and he called you by that name. I think it's rather cute. I wish Robert had a pet name for me."

"You do? He doesn't?"

Lisa and Rebecca laughed aloud. Lisa realized it felt good to laugh again. Her mood began to improve somewhat—and that was certainly a good thing.

Lisa changed the subject. "Rebecca, do you think Connie will be successful in her new venture?"

"I believe so. Christopher Creek is the perfect place for a new mercantile store … *and* a café. And, do you know what else I'm hoping for?"

"What?"

"That the entire Christopher Creek area will grow into a small community … and very soon."

"Why so?"

"Because if it does, the community will need to build a new schoolhouse, and we will be able to work closer to home!"

"Oh, I never thought of that. It would be nice to work closer to home. Our ride out here to Basin Flat *is* rather long."

"Oops, looks like we've gone past our allotted time for lunch. You round up the children, and I'll ring the bell," instructed Rebecca, officially ending their lunch break.

Within minutes, Lisa and Rebecca were back in their classrooms teaching the children their three *R*'s.

* * * * *

"Charlie, how long do you think it will be before construction starts on the new store?" Connie inquired of her newly hired building supervisor.

"When I was in Payson yesterday, I talked to the foreman at the lumber mill. He said he would have your lumber order filled by the end of next week … and would make delivery soon after that."

"That's grand. Were you able to grade any of the lumber? I'm hoping it's good quality."

"It all looked top-notch to me. And, you'll be happy to know that I have several men rounded up and ready to begin the construction as soon as the lumber is delivered. They'll be available on a moment's notice."

"I'm so excited, Charlie. I just feel in my heart that this venture will be well worth the effort and cost. Hopefully, by next spring, we'll be open for business."

"I have no doubt about that, Miss Lynne."

"Charlie, you've worked for my brother for nearly four years, and you've known me for more than two years, and yet you still refuse to call me Connie. Why is that?"

"Can't say fer sure, Miss Lynne. I reckon you can blame it on my up-bringing."

"Well, your mother would be proud of you."

"Thank you, ma'am. I believe she would be at that. God rest her dear soul."

* * * * *

At twenty minutes past eleven, Captain Williamson and his men reached the second way station—Carrizo Creek. Jess McCain was there to greet them. And he was not alone. The young ranger had brought another man with him to the rendezvous point. Neither McCain nor his companion looked old enough to shave—let alone be competent rangers.

"Greetings, gentlemen!" McCain said, rather jubilantly. "And, sir, would you be Captain Williamson?"

"I would be. And I *presume* you are Jess McCain?"

"Yes, sir. And this is Ranger Walt Eagar. He's been assigned to your detail, as well."

"Well, that's certainly good news. We can definitely use the extra help. Our mission is vital … and the more men we can muster, the better," Williamson declared.

After all the necessary introductions were made, the rangers gathered around Captain Williamson for another quick briefing. This was first-time information for the two new men—and they listened intently.

"Well, that's how I perceive it, men. Any comments?"

No one voiced an opinion. They just nodded in agreement to the captain's proposed plan.

"So be it! Now, tend to your horses, eat some lunch, and fill your canteens," instructed Williamson. "We'll take a slightly longer break at this station."

The allotted time for lunch seemed to hasten by. Forty minutes later the rangers were mounted and en route, once again, to Salt River Canyon. Their fate was just twenty-eight miles away. Each man felt the tension growing inside his gut.

Clint coaxed Liberty up alongside Williamson's big gelding. "Tom, do you think this gang of raiders might have a sentry or two posted around the upper rim of the canyon?"

"It's likely, Clint. I don't think we should get too close on this road. As we get nearer, we'll leave the roadway and circle around the rim just far enough to have a peek into the canyon. If any sentries are posted, we should be able to spot them, and hopefully take them out of action."

"Sounds like a good plan to me. What happens if they notice that their sentry is missing?"

"That's why we'll replace their man with one of our own. Hopefully, they'll think that *our* man standing atop the rim is one of their own."

"That ought to work out real good. So, when do we make our move to enter the canyon?"

"I'm hoping tonight … just after dark. We'll walk our horses down the steep trail and be in position near their camp by morning. With a whole lot of help from *above*, we'll take 'em by total surprise."

Clint reined Liberty back into line behind Blanco. It was going to be difficult getting into the canyon without being detected, even with the gang's spotters out of action and darkness concealing their approach.

Clint recalled a few cases in west Texas where he had to ride into a hidden canyon to seek out cattle rustlers. On one of those jobs he was shot in the leg. A sentry had been posted in just the right place, and he had failed to see him until it was too late. That mission failed. It would be another two months before he was able to ride after them again. The mission was successful the second time out.

* * * * *

When Lisa Wells—accompanied by Maree and Kris Reavis—returned home from her job at the school, she found Dusty Rhodes and Jenny Reavis sitting on the front porch. They were watching little Lena Wells as she played with some wooden blocks.

Maree and Kris leaped from the buggy, ran to their mother, and gave her a big hug. Kris turned to Dusty and gave him a hug as well. Maree—showing off her boldness—even went so far as to hop on Dusty's lap, wrap her arms around his neck, and plant a big kiss on his cheek.

"Well, young lady, how was school?" Dusty asked. "What new and interestin' thing did you learn today?"

"We read a wonderful storybook that Mark Twain wrote. Miss Lynne loaned the book to the school so our class could read it," Maree reported.

"I've heard of him. And just what would be the title of this Mark Twain book?" Jenny asked her daughter.

"*The Adventures of Tom Sawyer*," she quickly replied. "And it was the best story I ever heard!"

"Well, I'm glad you liked it. That was very nice of Connie to loan her book to the school," remarked Jenny, sincerely. "I may want to read it myself some day."

"I wouldn't mind readin' it, too," added Dusty.

Abruptly, Dusty turned his attention away from Jenny and the children and focused it on Lisa. He studied her face briefly, then said: "I reckon ya are wonderin' why I'm here at yore house?"

"Not really. I know about your relationship with Jenny. And just in case you are wondering … I approve. My only concern is, that you two don't get the *cart before the horse* … if you know what I mean. Or should I explain myself?"

"No ma'am—uh—I mean—yes, ma'am, I understand perfectly. I intend to marry Jenny as soon as I discuss the matter with my father. I shore hope he'll approve."

"I'm sure he will, Dusty. He knows that Jenny is a fine girl. I would think he would want his son to be happy. We'll invite him over for dinner tomorrow evening, and engage in a little family *pow-wow* afterwards."

"Lisa, I pray you are right in what you say," sighed Jenny, rather deeply. "I really do love Dusty."

"I know something about love, Jenny. I'm married to a wonderful man," Lisa happily confessed. "And I think it's great that *this time* you, too, will have a real chance to experience true love. I know full well that my brother, Ramon, wasn't the husband and father he should have been. He cared much more about his drinking than he did about you and the children."

Dusty began to reflect some signs of hope. "I do 'preciate yore support, ma'am. I think my father will listen to ya." He ended with an admission, saying: "I love Jenny very much."

Lisa swept Lena up into her arms, gave her a big hug, and kissed her chubby cheeks. Lena began to giggle.

"Jenny, let's get these children cleaned up, and start dinner. Dusty, won't you stay and join us. I'm sure that Jenny and the children wouldn't mind at all."

"Yes, ma'am, I'd like that very much."

Maree slid off Dusty's lap and headed straight for the front door—with Kris hot on her heels.

Jenny stood up, grabbed Dusty's arm, and pulled him from his chair. "Come on, cowboy!" she ordered.

Lisa began to inwardly contemplate as to where Jenny would be living after she married Dusty. *Will he be moving in with Jenny, here, at the Rim Shadow Ranch? Or would she and the children move in with Dusty?*

Lisa suddenly realized that there was one major problem: Dusty didn't have a home of his own. He was currently living with his father. It was certainly something that needed to be discussed in the coming weeks.

* * * * *

A shade before two o'clock, the rangers reached the Apache Springs way station. There, they quickly watered their horses and checked their gear. Fifteen minutes later they were moving southwest again. The rangers were making good time.

By four o'clock, they had arrived at North View, the final way station before descending into the canyon. The air temperature had risen significantly since leaving Show Low. Clint was glad that it wasn't mid-summer. The ride hadn't been all that bad—as far as the weather was concerned.

"Men," Williamson began, "it's not far from here to the rim of the canyon. We'll rest ourselves for about an hour. This would also be an opportune time to grab some grub, as well. We're gonna be real busy after we leave here. So enjoy this time out of the saddle while you can."

"I'm very surprised we got this far today," Clint commented to his boss.

"I'm glad we did," Williamson replied. Then he added, saying: "When you get a minute, Clint, let's interview the station manger and see if he has any pertinent information on these mangy *owl hoots* we're riding after."

The station manager was questioned for several minutes. He was fairly certain that the raiders were indeed hiding at the bottom of canyon—in a makeshift cabin about a mile downriver. He also informed the rangers that there was another way station at the bottom of the canyon, and that some of the raiders were staying there as well.

Captain Williamson immediately briefed his men on the new information.

Five o'clock came much too quickly. Captain Williamson summoned his rangers. "Time to go, men!

When they were about a mile from the canyon rim, Williamson steered his men off the roadway and sought out shelter among a grove of trees. Twenty minutes had elapsed since leaving the way station. The sun was slowly reaching downward toward the distant horizon.

"This looks to be a good spot for a temporary campsite," voiced Williamson. "We'll hold up here until it's nearly dark, and then I'll take one man with me to scout for sentries on the canyon rim."

The rangers made themselves busy setting up their campsite. The two packhorses were relieved of their burden.

"Sorry, men, but no campfire," instructed Williamson. "We can't give away our location."

After waiting for nearly an hour, Captain Williamson selected the new man, Jess McCain, to go with him to the rim of the canyon. They would ride to within a quarter-mile of the rim, then walk the rest of the way to the edge. It was imperative that they not be seen by any of the gang's sentries.

Fifteen minutes later, Williamson and McCain were "hunkered down" about one hundred yards from the rim of the canyon. And, just as they expected, a sentry was spotted sitting atop a large boulder where he could easily watch the north entrance to the canyon.

"Before we can begin our descent into the canyon, I've got to replace that sentry with you, Jess," Williamson whispered to his young recruit. "Hopefully, he'll give us some much-needed information on his gang … if we can take him alive."

"I'm ready, Captain. Ya want me to sneak up on him now?" asked McCain, with eagerness in his voice.

"Let's wait until the sun is a bit lower in the sky. I'm just hoping our sentry doesn't abandon his post before we have a chance to capture him."

Thirty more minutes elapsed. The sun was now partially hidden behind the distant horizon. The sentry had not as yet forsaken his post. The decision to advance was given.

"Jess, you go around to the right and come in behind him. I'm going back for my horse. I'll ride straight down the main road, and hopefully get him to focus his attention on me. When you see him checking *me* out … you take *him* out."

"Yes, sir!" replied Jess, reflecting self-confidence.

"Wait right here until I get to the roadway … otherwise he might spot you. It shouldn't take me more than five minutes to get into position."

Captain Williamson stealthily returned to his now anxious steed, mounted up, and reined his gelding carefully and quietly eastward toward the main road.

Jess checked his pocket watch. In five minutes he would go after his prey. He sucked in a deep breath and let it out slowly. Though feeling a bit nervous, disappointing his leader and comrades was not on his agenda.

At the roadway, Williamson checked his revolver before spurring Blanco southward. Now he tried to make as much noise as possible. As he got closer to the rim of the canyon, he even began to whistle a tune. Out of the corner of his eye he espied the sentry ducking behind a boulder closer to the roadway. He did not, however, spot his man, Jess McCain, from his present vantage point. He assumed that the young ranger was getting himself into position. At least he hoped so. Timing was everything now.

Jess could see the object of his pursuit just ten yards in front of him. The outlaw had his carbine leveled at the rider on the big white horse. It was now or never. He stealthily closed the gap between himself and his prey.

The young lawman was only nine short steps away from his intended target when the sentry heard him—and spun around. Jess charged at him with all his might. He slammed the man hard against the large boulder. The outlaw struck the back of his head with such force against the boulder that it knocked him out cold.

The spry lawman quickly climbed atop the boulder and signaled to his leader that he had taken full control of the lookout post. Williamson waved back, and reined his horse toward his successful ranger. In a couple of minutes he was dismounting next to his young recruit.

"Nice job, son. Did he give you any trouble?"

"No, sir," Jess began, "I rushed him so hard that he banged his head on that boulder. He's out cold."

"Let's disarm him … and get him tied up."

The two rangers wasted no time in securing the unconscious outlaw. Captain Williamson planned to take him back to the temporary campsite for interrogation.

"Ya better get up on that rock, Jess, and pretend you are this man. If someone down below looks up here and sees their sentry missing, well, I'm guessing they'll get nervous."

"Yes, sir."

"I'll ride out and fetch your horse. Keep a close eye on our prisoner. See ya in a couple of minutes."

After returning with Jess McCain's horse, Williamson retrieved the outlaw's mare. He unceremoniously tied the man across his own horse's saddle like a big bag of feed.

"I'm heading back to camp, son. You be careful."

Williamson rode back to camp—leaving his young ranger to takeover the sentry position.

Fifteen minutes later, Williamson rode into camp with his now conscious prisoner. Jim quickly assisted Williamson with the unloading of the outlaw. He was extracted from his saddle and tossed to the ground in a "not-so-gentle" manner.

"What ya have me to do with him, Captain?" asked Jim, in a gruff voice.

"I'd *prefer* to leave him tied up here in camp but, unfortunately, we'll have to take him into the canyon with us tonight. He would die up here all alone."

"You got a name, mister?" asked Clint, while poking the man hard in the ribs with the toe of his boot.

"Wo-Wo-Woods. For-For-Forrest Woods," he replied, fearing the next poke would break a rib.

"Say that again!" Clint fired back.

"For-Forrest Woods," he readily repeated. "My friends call me Woody."

"Well, we ain't yore friends," Will growled.

"Tom, what we have here," Clint began, "is the man that killed Ramon Reavis nearly two years ago!"

"Your wife's brother?" asked Williamson, to be sure he heard Clint correctly.

"Yes! He's the very same *hombre* that our fellow lawman, Marshal Chandler, has been searchin' for. And, there's a hefty reward for this man … and for his stinkin' partner too," Clint proclaimed.

"I ain't killed nobody, ranger!" Woods quickly yelled out. He feared that the rangers would hang him on the spot.

"Then who did?" Williamson demanded to know.

"I—I admit, I was there that night, but it was Ty Roper who stuck a knife in that feller," he hastily admitted. "I swear to you … I ain't never killed a livin' sole."

"Where can we find this *Roper*?" asked Clint, while grabbing at the man's shirt and pulling him closer.

"He's down in the canyon," replied Woods, his body now sweating profusely.

"Tell us what you know about the raiders … and I'll do my best to prevent you from hanging," Williamson promised.

For the next several minutes, the rangers interrogated their prisoner. He was most accommodating—spilling his guts with all he knew about the gang members and their operation.

"Well, men, the odds are better than I thought. I think we can handle ten men without too much trouble," Williamson speculated. "We've faced a lot worse odds."

"How long before we pull out, Captain?" Walt Eagar asked. He was feeling somewhat anxious to get underway.

"Well, we now know that Woods wasn't required to return to his camp until around nine o'clock … so that's when we will head down into the canyon," instructed Williamson.

"Reckon we got about an hour then," Jim announced.

"Men," Williamson began, "it will be dark soon. And thankfully, the moon will be nearly full tonight … and should be rising in the next hour. Now that we control the north lookout point, we haven't much to worry about between now and then. Reckon you can go ahead and build that campfire."

Within minutes, the crackling campfire was conquering the invading darkness around them. At a quarter to nine, Clint rode out to where Jess McCain was posted, and summoned him back to camp.

"As soon as Clint and Jess return, we'll break camp and head out," instructed Williamson.

By the time the campfire was extinguished, and everyone was ready to ride, it was a quarter past nine. The moon was just starting to peek over the distant mountain range.

"Well, men, are we ready to go?" Williamson asked.

He received an affirmative answer from each man.

Williamson turned to one of his young rangers, and said: "Walt, gag our prisoner and put him on his horse. If he so much as makes a peep … knock him out cold."

Clint could see the fear in Woods' eyes. He knew that the captain wasn't fooling. Clint guessed that they would have no trouble with their prisoner.

"Let's ride, men!" Williamson commanded.

This was the moment they had been preparing for. Soon, they would be descending into Salt River Canyon—in pursuit of the raiders.

Chapter Four

It was half past nine when the rangers started their slow descent into the deep canyon. The road was incredibly steep and narrow; with more twists and turns than a slithering Sonoran sidewinder.

"It's inconceivable to me, how a big ol' stagecoach is able to get down this blasted hill … and then of all things … climb back up the other side," commented Will, as he scratched his unshaven cheek.

"Good grief! I'm about to slide clean out of my saddle," proclaimed Jess, rather vociferously.

"Yeah! Me too!" echoed Walt.

"Guess we should have packed some glue!" added Jim, as he attempted to push himself rearward in his saddle.

Clint twisted around in his saddle and glanced back at his friends. "Do I need to tie you gents to your—"

"Gentlemen, please," Williamson cut in, "we've got to maintain some silence from this point on … so please, keep your banter to a whisper."

Nothing more was said until after they were nearly halfway down the treacherous hillside. Williamson was the first to break the silence, saying: "Men, we need to dismount and walk the rest of the way from here. A man on horseback is an easy target, and I don't aim to lose a single one of you … if I have anything to say about it."

"I'm all for that," whispered Jess, with a grin forming on his youthful face.

"Ya won me over, too, Captain," added Walt, as he hurriedly climbed down from his horse.

* * * * *

At the Rim Shadow Ranch, Lisa was busy grading papers and preparing the school lesson for the next day. Jenny and Dusty had retired to the front porch following the evening meal. Maree, Kris and Lena were all in their rooms—supposedly sleeping. Maree, on occasion, would sneak into Lena's room and play with her. Lisa was certain she could hear giggling coming from little Lena's room.

Tomorrow night, Dusty's father would be coming over for dinner. After the meal, Dusty and Jenny would announce their love for each other. Lisa hoped that it would all go well. She vowed to pray for them tonight before going to bed.

And retiring for the night was something that Lisa was not looking forward to. It would be another lonely night. While she was sleeping in a warm, comfortable bed, her man would be sleeping on the cold, hard ground under the stars.

Lisa began to consider how close the rangers were to finding the raiders. Then she recalled what Williamson had said: '*We ought to be in place by Wednesday*.' She suddenly realized that Clint and company could be in the *line of fire* as early as tomorrow. Her body shuddered at the thought of it, and she felt chills run up and down her arms.

Tonight she would pray for him and the other rangers harder than she ever had. She fully believed that God answered prayers. She had proof. All she had to do was look around at all she had. Her devoted husband was proof, Lena was proof, and the ranch was proof. She was truly blessed. Everything she had hoped and prayed for was a reality.

* * * * *

Cal Amarē, the leader of the raiders, was playing cards with several of his men in a small, ramshackle cabin that they had hastily assembled about a mile downriver from the Salt River Canyon way station. Most all of the materials used in building the cabin had been appropriated (at gun point) from several freight wagons that had attempted to pass through the canyon. Amarē and his men had been hiding out at this location for nearly three months. It had been at least two weeks since their last raid on some ranches just north of Globe.

"Hey, Cal, when are we gonna get outta here and do another job?" asked Doug Graves.

"Yeah! I'm sick and tired of sit'n 'round with nothin' to do," chimed in Cauble Stone.

"Stop yore whining. We gotta lay low for a good while. If Cole hadn't shot that rancher we'd not be holed up here this long," growled Amarē.

"Hey, it wasn't my fault! That rancher pulled a gun on me!" responded Cole Miner, in his own defense.

"Would y'all just play cards … and stop all this blasted arguing," lambasted Eddy Waters.

"By the way," Tull Oaks began, "where's Woody? He should have been back by now."

"Aw, he'll be along soon," remarked Harry Kahne, sourly. "He always was a bit slow at everything he ever did."

"Maybe he's over at the way station talkin' to ol' Aikey Hart," suggested Les Powers.

"Yeah. The last time he pulled watch he stayed overnight at the way station," said Waters, reminding everyone.

"Well, since you boys are so fired up to get out of here and find some excitement," Amarē began, "we'll ride out of here tomorrow … and pay a visit to the trading post over yonder at Jackson Butte."

"Hey, do ya think that purty little gal, Honey Combs, is still sell'n her *wares* down there at the tradin' post?" asked Miner, with a big grin on his face.

"Cole, you wouldn't know what to do with her *wares* even if she showed ya," teased Ty Roper.

"What do you know 'bout anything, Ty," Miner shot back.

"When's the last time you was with a woman?"

It appeared that Cole Miner was the underdog when it came to any conversation around the cabin. He was the youngest of the bunch—barely eighteen years old. He had never killed a man until that rancher tried to defend his property. After shooting him, Miner heaved up his guts for the best part of an hour. The older men had been pretty hard on him ever since.

Amarē slid his chair back from the table and stood up. "*Compañeros*, it's nearly ten o'clock. Let's call it a night. I think ol' Woody is probably sleeping over at the way station. We'll ride outta here sometime in the morning."

* * * * *

Captain Williamson and his men were now a "stone's throw" from the way station. A solitary light was faintly emanating from a small window at the back of the building. The din from the river was so thunderous that no one inside the station could possibly hear a single horse approaching, but someone inside just might hear *several* horses approaching.

"Hold up, men. This is close enough. We need to sneak on down there and see how many raiders we got holed up inside that building," instructed Williamson.

Clint did not hesitate. "I'll go! And I'll take Will with me … if he's game."

"I got your back, Clint. Let's get on down there," replied Will, enthusiastically.

Within five minutes, Clint and Will were peering in the dirty window from which the light was emanating. An elderly, heavy-set man was sitting on the edge of a bed—pulling off his soiled boots. He appeared to be alone in the tiny room.

"Could be that someone's bedded down in another room," whispered Will.

"I'm guessin' you're right 'bout that. When that fella extinguishes that lantern, we'll go around to the front door and ease our way inside."

"Sounds good to me, Clint," agreed Will.

Three minutes later, the room fell into darkness. The two rangers slipped stealthily around to the front porch—not because they could be heard above the din of the creek, but so as not to be spotted by someone peering out another window.

Will slowly lifted the wooden handle on the front door and eased it open as quietly as possible. When he entered, he spotted a man lying on a palette in the corner of the spacious front room. He tiptoed over to him and carefully slipped the sleeping man's gun from its holster and tucked the gun into his waistband. Meanwhile, Clint had positioned himself just outside the bedroom door.

When Clint gave the "ready" signal, Will went into action. He gave the man on the palette a brutal kick in the ribs. At the same exact moment, Clint kicked open the bedroom door. When the splintered door slammed against the wall it sounded almost like a gunshot.

The elderly man jerked violently, sat straight up in bed, and stared wide-eyed at Clint—who was standing near him with a revolver leveled at his heart. He threw his hands in the air and shouted: "Don't shoot mister, I ain't armed!"

"Stand up, slowly, and walk into the other room," commanded Clint, rather gruffly. As they exited the bedroom, Clint reached for the coal-oil lantern that was on the dresser.

Clint and his prisoner entered the front room, where Will was presently busy tying up his man. "Just 'bout got this *hombre* secured, Clint," announced Will, with a tone of satisfaction in his voice. "He decided to resist … so I had to bust him up the side of his head a couple of times."

"He looks plenty peaceful now," replied Clint, as he lit the lantern. "Now, let's find out who's who."

"I'll get this other lantern fired up so we can see even more clearly," said Will.

With the room now properly lit by the two lanterns, the rangers sized up their prisoners. "I haven't a clue which one is the station manager, but I'm reasonably certain that it's the one I pulled out of the bedroom," surmised Clint.

"I'd say you are probably right, Clint," Will agreed. "If you will keep 'em covered, I'll go get the captain and the rest of our crew."

When Clint nodded his head, Will bolted out the door and hustled up the road to where his boss and fellow comrades were waiting for a report.

"The building is secure, Captain. And we have two men in custody."

"Good job, Will," praised Williamson, with a smile on his face. "Men, when we get to the station, I want y'all to put your horses in the corral behind the building so they won't be easily spotted. Then spread yourselves out around the building … and keep your eyes peeled for trouble."

The rangers jumped into action. As soon as everyone was in his designated place, Williamson and Clowers entered the building and found Wells occupying a rocking chair with his prisoners sitting in a corner—bound and gagged.

"Hey, Clint," Williamson began, "did ya get any information out of these two *owl hoots*?"

"No, sir. I figured I'd wait until you got here."

"Will, please ask Jim to bring our other prisoner inside," requested Williamson. "Perhaps he can identify these two men."

A moment later, Jim O'Bryan and Will Clowers had their trembling prisoner, Forrest Woods, standing "front and center" in the presence of the captain.

"Okay, Woods, I want to know who these two are, and *pronto*!" demanded Williamson, in a rather harsh voice.

"That heavy-set fella is Gabby Smith, the manager of this here station. He's not a part of our outfit. That other fella is Aikey Hart … and he *is* one of our riders."

"Untie the manager, Will," Williamson ordered.

Gabby, as soon as his gag was removed, began cursing a blue streak. By the time his hands and feet were freed, he was even more livid—if that were possible.

"Gabby!" shouted Williamson. "Listen to me! If ya don't shut your yap, I'm gonna tie ya back up, and gag that filthy mouth of yours. Now what's it gonna be?"

Gabby immediately fell silent.

"Now … sit down over here at the table, Gabby, and I'll explain things to you," ordered Williamson, rather firmly.

Gabby, after receiving a brief explanation from the captain, seemed satisfied that his treatment had been necessary to protect the welfare of the Arizona lawmen.

Then Williamson turned about and addressed his men, saying: "Jim, take the first outside watch … and tell Walt and Jess to come on inside. Clint, I need you to continue guarding Woods and Hart. We'll rotate both duties every two hours."

Jim stationed himself outside, behind some rather large boulders, and not too far from the building. He sent Jess and Walt inside as instructed.

As soon as Jess and Walt entered the station, Williamson issued another order, saying: "The rest of you grab your bedrolls and get a couple hours of sleep. We've got to be at the raiders' hideout before sunrise."

Within thirty minutes, everyone that needed to be asleep was snoring away. Tomorrow would be a very trying day for the rangers. There was no doubt in Williamson's mind that most of the raiders would choose to *shoot it out* rather than surrender. He just hoped that none of his rangers would become a casualty in the fracas.

The one thing that pleased Williamson—for the moment at least—was having two of the raiders in custody. That meant two less guns firing on his men. The odds of survival were now much better. Williamson felt certain that new sentries would be coming up the river trail before sunrise. He needed to have his men in place, and ready to intercept them. Capturing two more raiders would greatly improve their survival chances.

As the night sped by, changes of the guard took place without a hitch. By five o'clock, everyone had gotten some sleep—though very little in a few cases. Regardless, it was time to get everyone up and ready to travel down river.

"I hate for us to travel on an empty stomach, men, but we don't have much time to get ourselves in place. I feel certain they will be sending sentries this way before it gets daylight. We've got to intercept them. It will improve our chances of defeating this gang of raiders."

"Hold on, Captain!" interjected Gabby. "It won't take me but a few minutes to brew some coffee beans and warm up a pan of biscuits for your men. I can do that while they is all git'n ready to travel."

"That's mighty nice of you, Gabby. Thanks," replied Williamson. "Okay, men, you heard him … get a move on! Coffee will be on the table by the time you collect yourselves."

"Woods, just how far away did you say that cabin of yours was from here?" Clint asked.

"Maybe less than a mile downstream. The cabin sets up against a canyon wall. No way to get in or out the backside. You'll only have three sides to worry about," responded Woods, without the necessity of Clint's boot being poked into his ribs again.

"Men, it looks as though we'll be leaving the horses here and walking in," instructed Williamson. "No sense getting our horses all shot up."

The aroma of coffee began to permeate the way station. In a matter of minutes, everyone would be gulping down a cup of the precious hot brew. Even the warm biscuits would be a welcomed treat.

Williamson turned and faced Walt. "Walt, I'm leaving you here to guard Woods and Hart. Keep 'em tied. If they want something to eat … shove a biscuit into their mouth."

"Not a problem, Captain!" Walt responded.

As soon as everyone had finished their coffee and had eaten a biscuit or two, Williamson gave the command, saying: "Men, let's move out!"

And may God be with us," Clint added. And to himself, he prayed: *Dear God, please place Your divine shield of protection around my friends and me this day. Amen.*

Chapter Five

Wednesday morning. Just a hint of sunlight was visible on the horizon by the time the rangers reached the makeshift cabin. They had encountered no one on the rocky trail to the hideout. That puzzled Williamson a great deal. He had fully expected new sentries to be sent up to the north and south rims. Suddenly it occurred to him: *Perhaps Woods and Hart were supposed to go back to the rim again as lookouts.*

While en route to the hideout, Williamson had instructed his men to stay out of sight and not to return fire until directed to do so. He wanted the raiders to think he was completely alone.

With many large boulders to choose from, the anxious rangers moved into position, covering three sides of the cabin with their carbines. Just as Woods had said, there was no exit out the rear of the cabin.

Williamson decided it was time for an early morning wakeup call. He aimed his carbine at one of the dirty front windows and squeezed the trigger. The roar echoing off the canyon walls was loud enough to wake the dead.

Several men could be heard shouting from inside the cabin. It even sounded like furniture was being knocked over. But no one came to the door or any of the windows to look outside. It got suddenly quiet inside the cabin.

Williamson now decided it was time to *verbally* declare himself. He yelled out: "You men inside the cabin! This is Ranger Williamson. You need to come out … unarmed … hands high in the air! I'm placing y'all under arrest!"

"What's goin' on ranger? Why ya here botherin' a poor ol' rancher like me?" Cal Amarē shouted.

"You ain't no poor rancher, mister! Two of your men are in custody as we speak … Woods and Hart!"

"I never heard of 'em! And I ain't comin' outside so you can shoot my dang head off!"

"I'm countin' to ten. If you ain't standin' outside with your hands in the air by then … I'm gonna fill that cabin with lots of lead." Williamson threatened.

Williamson never got the chance to count. Several windowpanes on the front side of the cabin were suddenly punched out. A hail of bullets quickly followed. Lead began ricocheting off the boulders that the rangers were using for their cover.

The raiders' horses—which were enclosed in a makeshift corral adjacent to the cabin—began to panic. They quickly knocked down a section of the corral fence. From that point on there was no stopping their escape. They ran fearfully upriver toward the way station.

Williamson signaled to his men to continue holding their fire, and to remain out of sight. He had to play out his little ruse just a while longer.

Just as quickly as the gunfire began—it stopped.

"What's the matter, ranger … ya got no bullets?" taunted one of the raiders.

"Hey, is ya all by yore lonesome out there, ranger?" asked another.

"Show yourself … and we'll chat a spell!" taunted another of the raiders.

"You'd best take me serious, gentlemen! You're trapped in there … and I'll *burn you out* if I have to!" Williamson bluffed.

"Well, I'll burn you with a bullet the moment you stick yore ugly mug up where I can see it!" Amarē yelled back.

"In case you *owl hoots* don't all ready know it … you haven't any horses. They're running half crazy up the trail!"

Seconds later, a window curtain was pulled back on the east end of the cabin—which faced the corral. It must have been a shock to the viewer that the horses were indeed gone—just as Williamson claimed.

"What did I tell you? You're on foot now! You had best come on out and give yourselves up! I'll give you two minutes to think it over!"

"Clint," whispered Williamson, "they truly believe I'm out here all alone. They haven't spotted any of you, yet. This could work to our advantage."

"How so, Tom?"

"I have a hunch that they will come charging out of there thinking that most, or all of them, will survive … and perhaps that one of them will get real lucky and kill me in the process," Williamson explained.

"I'll bet you're right, Tom," Clint agreed. "What a shock it will be when we *all* open up on them. I was hoping though that they would surrender."

"Yeah. Me too," sighed Williamson. "But ruthless men like them place no value on human life. They choose to live by a misguided code: *Kill or be killed*."

"It's a shame it has to be that way," Clint replied.

A minute or more passed by before Williamson addressed the gang of raiders again.

"What's it gonna be, gentlemen? Ya comin' out, or not?" Williamson shouted.

He quickly got his reply. Every gun in the cabin opened up on him again—but this time something else happened. Two men scrambled out the only door, and came running straight for him under the cover of gunfire emanating from the cabin. Williamson was hunkered down low, and didn't see them approaching, but Clint could see them from his concealed position.

Clint hurriedly leveled his carbine at the leading runner and fired. Les Powers stumbled forward six paces and fell face down on the hard earth. The second attacker stopped his straightforward advance and veered off to one side—right into the gun sights of Jim O'Bryan.

Harry Kahne didn't feel the hard earth as his body smashed onto it. He was dead before his knees began to buckle. The bullet from Jim's carbine had pierced his heart.

It was now obvious to Cal Amarē that Williamson was not working alone. He had just lost two of his men in quick succession. He was now certain that at least one other ranger was outside the cabin.

The shooting subsided once again. Amarē yelled out to Williamson, asking: "What kinda game you playin' out there, ranger?" Then he said: "You lied about bein' all alone!"

"I never lied … you just *assumed* that I was alone!"

"So, just how many men you got lurkin' out there?"

"Why don't you come on out and see for yourself!"

At that moment, a window on the west side of the house was pushed opened. Seconds later, a skinny, and rather young looking raider dove headlong out of the window and tumbled several times on the ground. Then, like a frightened deer, he was swiftly on his feet and running downstream with all his might. Jim fired two shots at him. Both missed.

This concerned Williamson. A raider was now roaming freely about who could get a bead on one of them. Something had to be done—and fast. Williamson motioned for the young and nimble Jess McCain to go after the fleeing outlaw.

Jess immediately leaped from his secure position and chased after the fleeing fugitive. The other rangers provided cover for him by firing a hail of bullets through the windows of the cabin until their man was out of danger.

"I hope Jess can catch up to that kid," Williamson said.

"Jess is young. If anyone can chase him down, it will be him. I certainly don't think you or I could get it done. Sorry, Tom, but that's the truth," proclaimed Clint, with a chuckle.

"My best guess is that we've still got six raiders inside that cabin to deal with. Doesn't look to me like anyone is gonna come out peacefully," Clint surmised.

"No … not at all. I think burning them out just might be the answer to our dilemma, after all. Ya see all that hay over in the corral? If we could set fire to it … it would spread to the cabin in a few short minutes."

"Tom, that's fifty yards away! How we gonna toss a burning match that far?" Clint asked.

"See that ledge just above the cabin? Well, if a man climbed up there, he could set a rag on fire, and drop it straight down on that hay," Williamson explained.

"And I know a sucker that can do it. Me!" Clint proclaimed. "Give me some cover fire … and I'll beat a path over to those rocks that lead up to the ledge."

From his hiding place, Clint studied the ledge and looked for the safest possible route in getting there. He quickly realized that a safe route didn't exist. No matter how wide a circle he made, he could still be seen from the cabin windows.

Clint propped his carbine against the boulder he was hiding behind and got himself ready for a fifty-yard dash. He turned and faced his boss and said: "I guess it's now or never, Tom. Let's get this over with."

Williamson signaled to Will and Jim to open fire on the cabin one more time. As they were firing, Clint ran to the spot he had previously chosen. Seconds later, he was in place, and ready to scale the wall of rock. It looked simple from far away, but now, standing under the ledge, it seemed impossible.

It took several attempts, but Clint finally managed to reach the precarious ledge. He carefully sidestepped his way along the narrow outcropping until he was standing directly above the corral—and the pile of hay. He knew he had only one shot at getting it right. He reached into his hip pocket, extracted his handkerchief, and tied a small stone inside it—to give it some weight. He extracted a match from his shirt pocket, lit it, and held it to the handkerchief. As soon as it was fully engulfed in flames, he dropped the fiery piece of cloth toward the dry hay, which was fifteen feet below him.

It took about twelve seconds for the hay to ignite. When it did, the flames quickly reached high into the air—almost to where Clint was standing. The fire quickly spread to the wooden fence posts and railings, and finally to the cabin. The smoke was thick, and as black as tar.

"Get ready, men!" Williamson shouted. "They ought to be feeling toasty any minute now!"

Clint was hurrying as fast as he could to get down from the ledge. The thick smoke from the fire was nearly blinding him. The last thing he desired was to be trapped on the ledge in full view of the raiders.

Gunfire erupted once more. Williamson cautioned his men to conserve their ammunition. "Wait for a clear shot!"

The fire spread up the east wall of the cabin—igniting the roof. It wouldn't be long now before the fire and smoke would drive the raiders from their lair.

Like his *partner-in-crime* had done before him, Tull Oaks bailed headfirst out of the open west-facing window. However, it didn't turn out quite the way he had it planned. The problem being: He was exceedingly more than six-feet tall, weighed over two hundred pounds, and was forty years old. He was nowhere near as agile as the skinny young man who earlier had bailed from the cabin window.

Will fired twice at the fleeing man. His second shot found its mark. Oaks toppled forward in a heap—dropping his revolver. He tried to get back up, but the nasty wound in his lower thigh said otherwise. He crawled over to a boulder and sat with his back up against it. Pulling a bandana from around his neck, he tied it above his wound to stop the bleeding. He made no further attempt to escape.

The cabin was now filled with choking black smoke and raining hot embers. The roof was heavily engulfed in flames. In a matter of moments it would probably collapse on top of the remaining raiders. They would have to get out or burn to death. The rangers were counting on the former.

From far downriver, the rangers could hear gunfire. It seemed apparent that Jess had caught up with the young escapee. They all hoped it was going well for Jess.

At that moment, the door of the cabin burst open, and five men came running out with guns blazing. It was obvious that this would be their *waterloo*. Jim fired first, taking out Eddy Waters. Will got a bead on Cauble Stone, and squeezed the trigger. Cauble grabbed his chest, stood perfectly still for nearly five seconds, and then crumpled to the rocky ground.

Clint, now secure in his former hiding place, managed to get a couple of rounds squeezed off at Cal Amarē. The bandit leader miraculously ducked every round, and was now safe behind a large boulder to Clint's right.

Doug Graves took a bullet in the shoulder, but still managed to run downstream about seventy yards before seeking cover behind a pile of boulders.

The last man to exit the inferno was Ty Roper. The back of his shirt was on fire. He dropped to the ground and began rolling over and over—finally extinguishing the flames. Jim thought he would lie there, perhaps surrender, but not so. Roper sprang to his knees, pointed his weapon at Williamson, and fanned the hammer on his revolver as quickly as he could. After four missed shots the hammer fell on spent cartridges.

"Give it up, mister!" yelled Jim, stepping out from behind his hiding place. "You can't possibly win this one!"

Jim's words fell on deaf ears. For Roper quickly slipped his last two remaining cartridges into his revolver. Seeing the danger that was about to unfold—Jim raised his carbine and pulled the trigger. The result was terrifying. For all Jim heard was a deafening *click*. His carbine was empty!

Roper twisted around on his knees and pointed the muzzle of his six-shooter directly at Jim. At that same precise moment, a shot from Williamson's carbine stopped him in mid-action. Ty Roper dropped his revolver, looked down at the hole in his chest, and fell forward—dead.

Seeing that he had no means of escape, Cal Amarē tossed his gun out into the open. He bellowed out at the top of his lungs, saying: "I give up! Stop your shooting!"

"Come out, so I can see ya!" Clint ordered.

Amarē hastily stood up and walked out into the open. Clint immediately approached him, checked him for additional firearms, and then tied his wrists together.

"I got this man secured, Tom!" Clint reported.

"Good work, Clint! I'll check on these others. It appears most of them are done for!"

Will approached the wounded Tull Oaks. The man made no effort to resist. "What's yore name, mister?"

"O-Oaks—T-Tull Oaks," he barely managed to say. "I'm h-hurt real bad, ranger."

"I'll get ya fixed up soon," said Will, as he picked up the man's revolver and tucked it into his waistband.

Jim headed downstream in search of the second man that had fled in that direction, but he stopped in his tracks when he heard gunfire.

"Someone's still shootin' at us, Captain!" Jim yelled.

At that moment, Jess McCain appeared from behind some rocks. "Hey, it's me! Don't shoot!" he yelled.

"What was all the shootin' 'bout?" Jim asked.

"There was a fellow hidin' down there in the rocks. When I saw him level his revolver at you, I fired a couple of rounds at him," Jess answered.

"Is he dead?" Jim asked.

"Very!" came the reply.

Captain Williamson immediately inquired of the young McCain, asking: "How 'bout that other fella you chased after? Did you catch up to him?"

"Yes … and no. I got real close. We exchanged a few rounds, but I'm afraid he gave me the slip, sir. I'm really sorry," Jess apologized.

"No need to apologize, son," Williamson replied.

"The good news is … I think he's out of ammunition," Jess added.

Chapter Six

Captain Williamson had gotten his men and the two prisoners well away from the burning cabin—which was nothing but smoldering embers now. It was consumed by fire faster than a ravenous cowboy putting away a juicy steak.

Thankfully, none of the rangers had been injured in the gun battle. However, the same could not be said for the raiders. Of the nine men at the cabin: six were killed, one was badly wounded, one surrendered, and one got away.

Williamson learned two things from his interrogation of the men he now had in custody: Cole Miner, a lad of eighteen years, was the raider who had escaped; and that Miner had killed a rancher near Globe.

It made Williamson very happy to know that he had the leader of the raiders in custody. He was not familiar with the name, Cal Amarē, but he was reasonably certain that somewhere in Arizona, someone was looking to hang the man.

Tull Oaks was seriously wounded, and would not be able to walk back to the way station. Williamson again turned to his youngest man, Jess McCain, and asked him to fetch a horse from the way station. Jess obeyed without a fuss.

Thirty minutes had elapsed by the time Jess came riding up on his own mare. Three more horses were in-tow. Obviously, not enough horses for everyone to ride out on.

"Where d'ya find them three nags?" Jim asked.

"Found 'em up near the way station. Reckon they belong to these raiders. Hope we got saddles for 'em."

"I saw two or three unburned saddles over by the corral," Will said.

"Good. Saddle up these nags and get yourselves outta here," Williamson ordered.

Soon, the three horses *of questionable breeding* were saddled. Because of his injury, Tull Oaks was hoisted aboard one of the nags. Jim and Will mounted the other two remaining nags. Jess remained aboard his personal mare. Cal Amarē would have to walk back to the way station.

"Men, Clint and I will wait here until you return with our horses. We'll keep ourselves entertained by moving these corpses over to that area near the corral. Can't have them lying too close to this here river … foul'n up the water."

As the others rode off, the two remaining rangers made good on their efforts to move the bodies to the corral. It was disgusting work, but someone had to do it.

Rangers Williamson and Wells were perched on a pile of rocks near the river—resting their aching backs—when Jim rode in with their horses. They were glad to see him.

"Did you two *old men* get them raiders transplanted to a better place?" asked Jim, with a chuckle.

"Yeah. We got er done. And, *mister*, you ain't that much younger than us!" countered Williamson, with a bit of snippiness in his voice.

"Ya got that right!" Jim quickly confessed.

"No doubt in *my* mind," teased Clint, grinning.

"Say, Captain, ya just gonna leave them fellas stacked all neat-like over there?" Jim asked.

"Reckon so, Jim. We haven't a wagon, or any extra horses to use in hauling them out of here. If time allows … and I don't think it will

… we might come back later and pile some rocks over 'em."

"Perhaps Gabby has a useful idea as to how we can solve this dilemma," Clint said.

"If it were up to me … and I know it ain't … I'd leave 'em just like they are!" Jim declared. "The coyotes will take care of the problem!"

"Well, don't think for a minute that I haven't considered it!" Williamson confessed.

* * * * *

From a safe distance, Cole Miner had been carefully observing Williamson and Wells as they stacked the bodies of his comrades near the corral. He would have gladly shot them both if it were not for the fact that he was out of ammunition. He had spotted two revolvers lying in the dust near the remains of the cabin, but he was wise enough to know that he would never be able to get to them without being spotted—and most likely killed.

Any future attempt by Miner to get his hands on one of those revolvers came to an abrupt end when Clint collected those guns—and several others that were lying about. He also rounded up the holsters and all ammunition belts he could find. A carbine was found in the ashes of the cabin, but it had been severely damaged by the fire. Clint left it where it was.

Miner watched as the three rangers rode off. He knew he had to follow them. There was no other way out of the canyon without going many miles downstream. Without a horse, it would be suicide. Perhaps he would come across his own horse wandering near the way station. He certainly hoped so.

* * * * *

At the way station, Williamson gathered his men around him and congratulated each one personally. He was very proud of the way they had performed their duties.

Gabby spent several minutes patching up Tull Oaks' leg. He felt certain that the bullet had shattered the bone. The bleeding had stopped, so the pressure on the tourniquet was slowly released. The bleeding did not resume. Gabby poured some of his rotgut whiskey on the wound to sterilize it before making a splint for the leg.

"This whiskey ought'a kill every germ known to mankind," Gabby proclaimed.

No one doubted him.

As soon as Gabby was finished, Oaks was retied and placed in the corner of the room with his three friends.

"Gabby, we've got lots of grub out back on our packsaddles, so … if we brought some of it in, would you fix us all up with some lunch?" Williamson asked.

"Be more 'n glad, Captain!"

Williamson turned about and addressed his rangers, saying: "Men, after you've eaten … grab a short nap. I'll keep an eye on these *owl hoots* for a while. I still need to glean some more information from them … especially, the names of those that didn't survive this morning's shootout. Somewhere, there's a lawman wanting to know their current status."

Gabby served up a most scrumptious meal. Everyone ate his fill. Most were now ready for that nap.

"Well, I'm more hot and dusty than sleepy. That river water might be cold, but I'm gonna take a dip in it just the same," Jess remarked. "I'll see ya fellas in a bit."

Williamson spent his post-meal time collecting information from Cal Amarē. The leader of the raiders was very forthcoming with the names of the deceased. A wanted poster would be requested on Cole Miner as soon as they got back to Show Low. That would be a task for Sheriff Hannagan.

Satisfied that the interrogation had gone well, Williamson looked around to see where everyone had gone. Will and Walt were snoozing in the far corner of the room on their bedrolls, Clint was in the kitchen helping Gabby wash dishes, and Jim was on the porch napping in a hammock. He recalled that Jess was going to the river for a refreshing dip.

"Clint, if you're not planning on resting your eyes … would ya mind keeping an eye on these *owl hoots*? I believe I could use a few winks before we head out."

"Not a problem, my friend. You go ahead and grab some shuteye," replied Clint, as he moseyed over to the big padded rocking chair and sat down. *Might as well be comfortable while I'm on guard duty*, he thought to himself.

Williamson strolled to the far corner of the room and stretched out on his bedroll. He was snoring away in less than two minutes.

Not twenty minutes had elapsed when a gunshot could be heard—startling almost everyone to full alertness. Jim sat up so fast that he tumbled out of the hammock—landing facedown on the porch floor. When he looked up he saw a man riding south at a full gallop. He was aboard Jess' horse.

Walt was the first person to exit the building, followed closely by Captain Williamson. Will hadn't budged. He was apparently a sound sleeper. Clint could only go as far as the front door and peer outside. He was not about to abandon the prisoners.

Just then, Will—who was somewhat awake—asked: "Hey, Clint, what's goin' on?"

"Will, on your feet! Hurry, man! Watch these men for a minute! Okay? There's trouble! I have to assist Tom!"

With Will now fully alert, Clint dashed out the door, and ran to the backside of the way station. He didn't like what he saw. Jim and Walt were fishing Jess out of the water. He had been shot dead. There was no doubt in anyone's mind who the killer was—a young kid by the name of Cole Miner.

"Did you recognize the rider, Jim?" asked Williamson, his hands noticeably shaking.

"Yes, sir. It was that blasted kid that Jess was chasing earlier this morning. He must have doubled back. Jess' gun and holster were over there on that boulder … but they're gone now. That means the kid is fully armed again."

Williamson rushed forward with a plan, saying: "Clint, you and I have the two fastest horses here. We'll take after him riding atop horses that belong to them *owl hoots* we have in custody.

"We'll *tow* our good horses up that steep canyon road. And when we get to the top, we'll abandon the nags and mount our hearty steeds.

"That mare Miner took will most likely be plum worn out when she gets to the top of that steep grade. We should be able to run her down in no time at all."

"Great idea, Tom. Let's get moving!"

The rangers quickly saddled their steeds. The two nags were already saddled. Before anyone had a chance to say a word, they were gone in a cloud of dust.

The road up the south wall of the canyon had nearly as many switchbacks as the north road. The nags were puffing and wheezing most all the way to the top. Liberty and Blanco seemed to take it all in stride. Not being burdened by a rider made all the difference.

It took a considerable amount of time to cover the four and half miles, but the two rangers soon topped out over the rim. They quickly switched to their own horses. Liberty and Blanco raced forward like two bolts of sizzling lightening. Clint felt like the two horses were competing with each other to see who was the swiftest.

It didn't take long to catch up with the young fugitive. He was now barely a quarter-mile ahead of them, and the gap was closing rapidly.

Miner turned around in his saddle and fired a couple of quick shots at his pursuers. Both shots, fortunately, missed their intended targets. Clint and Williamson did not try to return fire. They were totally focused on running down the galloping horse that was ahead of them.

Less than a quarter-mile further, Jess' stolen mare stumbled and fell headfirst—rolling over and over several times before coming to a rest. She had run her last.

Miner survived the fall. Dazed, he stood up and quickly checked himself for injuries. The blood now dripping from his chin was coming from his broken nose.

His revolver had flown from his hand and was somewhere in the brush. With the rangers only fifty yards away, and approaching at a determined pace, he scrambled to find it.

Clint brought Liberty to a sliding halt, bailed out of the saddle, and ran to where Miner was reaching down for the dropped six-shooter.

Just as the young outlaw twisted about to fire the dusty revolver,

Clint drew his Colt. In the time it takes to blink an eye, Clint's .44-.40 barked with an ear-shattering roar. The big, heavy bullet was instantly speeding to its target.

Miner spun around hard, dropped his weapon, and fell face forward—his body crashing down onto a large prickly-pear cactus. Blood was rapidly staining the middle of his shirt.

Williamson walked over, knelt down beside the bloody body, and checked for any signs of life. There was none.

"Why do you suppose this kid has so much blood all over his clothes?" Williamson asked.

"Take a look at Jess' mare. She was bleeding badly from her nose just before she collapsed. I'd say it was spraying back on the kid," Clint speculated.

"Ya know what, Clint? I'm really sorry that that mare had to die for the likes of this *maggot*. Jess really cared a lot for that little mare."

"I'll get my rope and drag her off the roadway."

Moments later, Clint slipped the loop around the mare's neck and tied the other end to his saddle horn. He slowly pulled the mare into a grove of small trees.

Williamson, meanwhile, emptied out Miner's pockets and stripped him of Jess' holster. He gathered up Jess' dusty gun and slid it into the holster. After fetching his own horse, Blanco, he deposited the gun and holster in his saddlebag.

Clint returned to the roadway and addressed his boss, saying: "I had to cut the broken saddle off the mare. I did manage to salvage the halter, bridle and saddlebags."

"That's good, Clint. Now help me tote Miner's carcass over there … near the mare. We'll pile some rocks on him. Can't very well leave him at the edge of the roadway for the nice folks on the stagecoach to see."

Williamson sighed heavily as they were lowering Miner's body into a slight natural depression in the earth. He glanced over at the mare, and said: "I just hope the *mare* will forgive us for placing this murdering *skunk* on the same side of the road that she's on."

Clint started laughing. In fact, he laughed so hard that his sides started to hurt. "That's funny!" he managed to say.

"Gee, Clint, it wasn't *that* funny … was it?" Then he started to laugh too. The stress had finally gotten to them, and they had to let it all out.

Miner was hurriedly buried under a large pile of rocks. The busted saddle was placed on top of the rocks—as a marker, so to speak. The mare's halter and bridle were put in Williamson's saddlebag next to Jess' gun and holster.

Clint secured Jess' saddlebags over the top of his own.

After allowing Liberty and Blanco to rest a short while longer, Clint and his boss mounted up and rode north—back toward the canyon and way station.

"Do you think Jess has someone special waiting for him back at Fort Apache?" Clint asked.

"I don't know, Clint. He never mentioned anyone. He might have family living somewhere near the fort."

"I'll bet Walt would know," Clint surmised.

"Yeah. Maybe so." Tom paused a second or two, then added, saying: "Clint, let's round up those two nags we rode up here on and take them back with us. We'll certainly need 'em for the trip back to Show Low."

"Yes, Tom, I'm sure you're right 'bout that."

Neither ranger said anything more as they rode back to the way station at the bottom of the canyon. Both were reflecting on the loss of Jess McCain. The young ranger had made the ultimate sacrifice. He would be greatly missed.

Chapter Seven

Gabby guided Will and Jim to a place where they could bury Jess McCain. It was a flat, elevated plot of land on the south bank of the Salt River. Gabby assured them that even the highest water levels would not disturb the resting place of their comrade. Walt remained at the way station to guard the prisoners. He was glad he didn't have to watch his friend being buried. He thought to himself: *I should have gone along with the captain to help catch the mangy coward that shot Jess.*

Jess' burial had been completed by the time Clint and Captain Williamson returned to the way station. The two rangers dismounted in front of the station and tied their horses—along with the two nags—to the sturdy hitching rail. Liberty and Blanco seemed to be in good condition despite the recent ordeal of having ascended the canyon in record time, and then running at top speed for nearly a mile.

Williamson—after entering the station—addressed Eagar: "Walt, does Jess have any family over at Fort Apache?"

"Yes, sir. There's an older brother."

"Would you accompany me outside? I want to give you Jess' things. I'd like for you to take them to his brother."

"Yes, sir," Walt said. "I'd be more 'n glad to do that."

The two men walked outside onto the porch. Walt was the first to speak, asking: "Uh, sir, where's Jess' horse?"

"Miner killed the mare. Ran her plum to death. The saddle was badly damaged when she fell … and not worth haulin' back," Williamson explained. "Sorry."

"I understand, sir," Walt replied. "And, sir, we went ahead and buried Jess while y'all was away. I hope it was okay that we didn't wait for your return? I can show you where we buried him, if ya like."

"Not a problem, Walt. You can show me later."

And it wasn't a problem. Williamson was grateful that he didn't have to participate in the burial of another of his men. It would have been more than he could bear. He thought back to the burial of rangers Bud Wilcox and Chuck Carson, and how difficult that had been for him.

Williamson gave Walt all of the salvaged items. Walt quietly gathered them into his arms and re-entered the station. Williamson, however, sat down on the porch steps. He was exhausted. He thought: *I'm git'n way too old for this.*

Clint came out onto the porch and announced that coffee was being served.

"Thanks, Clint."

"You feelin' all right, Tom?"

"I reckon. A whole lot less excitement and a good night's sleep would be mighty nice."

"That goes for both of us!" declared Clint, as he and Williamson entered the station.

Before going outside the station to have a smoke, Will addressed his boss, asking: "Just when are we pulling out of this here noisy canyon, Captain?"

"I'd say in the next hour or two, Will."

"Yer all invited to spend the night," Gabby interjected. "I know this ain't much of a hotel, but yore more 'n welcome to it. I'd enjoy the company."

"Thanks, Gabby," Williamson began, "but we need to be kicking up some trail dust. We'll spend the night somewhere atop the north rim. That way, come morning, we'll have a fairly level shot most of the way to Show Low."

"And a bit drier, too. That high-desert country can be purty warm yet this time of year … but it'll be plenty cool by the time ya get to the pine country," Gabby reasoned.

"Gabby, I've been meaning to ask you … does the stagecoach still run by here?" Clint asked.

"Not fer some time now. Them raiders put a halt to most of the traffic 'round here. I've been low on supplies for quite a spell. I had to take the team horses out of here 'bout a month ago. Had no feed to give 'em."

"When we get back to Show Low, we'll let the stage company know that things are pretty much back to normal around here," Williamson promised. "Hopefully, you'll see a supply wagon down here in the next couple of days."

"That shore would be nice!" Gabby exclaimed.

An hour had passed when Williamson made his announcement, saying: "Men, it's time to ride out of here. Let's get our stuff packed up, and these prisoners on their horses.

"And, Gabby, we're gonna leave you some canned goods to get you by until that freight wagon shows up here."

"Much obliged, Captain!"

"More than glad to do it, Gabby … especially after what we've put you through," Williamson concluded.

Forty-five minutes later, the rangers pulled out onto the roadway, and started up the steep, four-mile incline leading to the north rim of Salt River Canyon.

Williamson had been thankful when two more of the raiders' horses wandered by the way station just as they were preparing to leave; otherwise, a couple of the prisoners would have had to ride double. Since there were no more serviceable saddles, the worse thing now was that one of the prisoners would be riding bareback. It was the captain's plan to give each prisoner his turn on the barebacked horse.

Three hours later, the weary party stopped at the North View way station just long enough to water their horses and check their gear. The rangers wanted to bivouac at North View, but Williamson elected to go on to the next station.

Sunset was close at hand by the time the rangers reached the Apache Springs way station. Here they would find the water *and* feed they needed for their horses.

"Men," Williamson began, "I want y'all to take extra special care of your horses tonight. They've had a rough day of haul'n our beefy hind ends out of that canyon."

"I'll rustle up some firewood and get a campfire started before it gets dark," said Clint, volunteering as usual.

"Let me give you hand with that chore, Clint."

"Thanks, Will. I can always use an extra pair of hands," responded Clint, with a slap to Will's shoulder.

"My appreciation to both of you," said Williamson, as he looked about the newly established camp.

As Clint and Will walked off into the high-desert terrain in search of dry wood, Williamson turned about and addressed Jim, saying: "My friend, I believe it's your turn to cook for us starving chow-hounds. Am I right or wrong?"

"Yeah. I'm thinkin' yore right 'bout that, sir."

Darkness was closing in by the time the horses were properly cared for and the campsite was fully operational. Dinner was soon being served.

"Beans and more beans!" Aikey Hart complained.

"Shut up and eat, or go hungry!" Jim countered.

"Better enjoy them beans, boys. I hear at Yuma prison they only serve bread and water," added Will, with a smirk.

"Ha! Ha! Says you!" replied Cal Amarē, snidely.

"I've got good news for ya, boys. I hear tell that on Sunday you get meat. Rattlesnake!" Clint chided.

"When we get these *yahoos* delivered to Hannagan in Show Low … I'm orderin' me a big ol' steak at the Blue Moon Café," Jim declared.

"Well, speakin' fer right here and now … these beans is just fine with me. I was git'n so hungry that I was near ready to chew the pads off a prickly-pear cactus!" commented Will, sounding as though he was indeed serious.

Everyone laughed. They had to. It was either that or cry. It had been a horrific day for each of them. The worst part was the outright cold-blooded murder of Jess McCain. He would be remembered—always.

* * * * *

At the Rim Shadow Ranch, everyone was sitting at the dinner table finishing the last of their delicious meal that Lisa and Jenny had prepared.

Besides Lisa, Jenny, and the three children, there were their honored guests—Dusty Rhodes, and his father, Charlie. Unknown to Charlie, this meal was a "setup" so that Dusty could tell his father about his involvement with Jenny.

"Mighty fine meal, ladies. Enjoyed it immensely," proclaimed Charlie, while sucking at his teeth.

"Glad you enjoyed it, Mister Rhodes," Jenny replied.

"Y'all adjourn to the living room for some conversation," Lisa directed. "I'll serve coffee in a few minutes."

"Can I help you, ma'am," Dusty asked. He was hoping to delay the revelation he had planned for his father.

"Not a chance! Now get yourself in there and relax," Lisa chided. "I'll be in there in ten minutes."

"Yes, ma'am," Dusty replied. He reluctantly obeyed.

Dusty joined his father, Jenny, and the children in the living room. He was so nervous he didn't know if he could keep his dinner down. He just wished that Lisa would hurry up and join the group.

"Well, Mister Rhodes, did you get enough to eat?" Lisa asked. She promptly planted herself down on the sofa and immediately cuddled up to him.

"W-why, yes, Mrs. Wells, I certainly did."

"I'm so glad," Lisa began, "because I hate to discuss *business* on an empty stomach."

"Business? What *business*?" asked Charlie, his face reflecting a high degree of confusion.

"The business of *marriage*, of course!" Lisa blurted out. She grabbed his arm and squeezed it firmly.

"W-whoa, Mrs. Wells … you is already married!"

"And if I wasn't?" asked Lisa, coyly.

Charlie's face turned as red as a beet. "I—I refuse to answer that question, Mrs. Wells. I don't need no trouble from yore husband."

"I'm just mess'n with you, Mister Rhodes," confessed Lisa, with a giggle. "But you *are* a handsome man. Did you know that? I'm sure if you wanted to get hitched, you'd have no problem finding a nice woman."

"Uh—y-yes, ma'am. I suppose. Are ya wantin' to fix me up with someone in particular? Say, someone like Mrs. Myers … or yore friend in Globe … Mrs. Day?"

"Heavens, no, Mister Rhodes! I wouldn't be up to any such thing. Besides, they are too old for you."

Lisa had her opening, and pressed forward. "But you do agree, Mister Rhodes, that everyone ought to have someone *special* in his or her life to call their own?"

"Uh, yeah. I reckon everyone needs someone."

"Well said, Mister Rhodes. I perfectly agree."

"Mrs. Wells, is there a *point* to this conversation?"

"Yes, Mister Rhodes. Indeed there is."

"Would ya mind let'n *me* in on it?"

"Sitting in this very room is an energetic young man and a pretty young woman who just happen to be in love, Mister Rhodes. And that young man has something burning in his heart that he needs to share with you," Lisa explained.

"Is that right, son?"

"Y-yes, sir," confessed Dusty, stepping on his words.

"Well, spell it out for me, son," Charlie demanded.

"Sir, Miss Jenny and I are—er—we're in love," Dusty began, "and we want yore permission to get hitched."

"Ya don't say! Well, if that doesn't beat all! I had a feelin' that somethin' was goin' on … especially since you was comin' home late most nights."

Lisa couldn't resist commenting on the lovebirds. "Isn't love a wonderful thing, Mister Rhodes?"

Charlie looked at Lisa, but made no reply to her comment. He quickly turned back to face his son. "So ya want my permission, huh? May I think on this matter for a spell?"

"That would be fine, sir," agreed Dusty, though wishing for his father's answer right then and there. But he would not disrespect his father. He loved him too much to do that. After all, the man did all he could to raise him alone after his mother died.

"Well," Lisa began, while taking in a deep breath, "let me prepare another pot of fresh coffee. Jenny, would you mind helping me? Please."

"Yes, ma'am. I'd like very much to help." She spoke a half-truth. Removing herself from the tension in the living room was her primary motivation.

"Mrs. Wells," Charlie began, "Dusty and I are gonna go outside for a moment. We'll be right back."

"That will be fine, Mister Rhodes. Take all the time you need," Lisa replied.

After Charlie and Dusty departed, Lisa glanced at Jenny and saw the tears welling up in her eyes. Lisa gave her a gentle hug, and spoke in a consoling voice, saying: "It's gonna be just fine, Jenny. You'll see. Show some faith."

"Oh, how I want to believe that. Didn't you see the look on Mister Rhodes' face when Dusty told him about me?"

"Yes, I saw it. Probably, I would have been in shock, too. But that doesn't mean he will disapprove," Lisa reasoned.

Nearly twenty minutes elapsed by the time Charlie and Dusty returned to the living room. It was difficult to discern what the outcome had been from their private talk—for each well-tanned face displayed a blank expression.

"Gentlemen, please join us at the table for some freshly brewed coffee," announced Lisa, hoping to break the tension.

"Dusty walked into the kitchen and stood behind Jenny. He reached out and put his hands on her shoulders. "I'd like to make an announcement," he began, "this here lady is gonna be my wife."

Jenny gasped, slumped in her chair, and looked as though she would faint. But she recovered quickly.

"Congratulations to the both of you!" shouted Lisa, smiling from ear-to-ear. "And congratulations to you, Mister Rhodes, because you are getting a fine daughter-in-law!"

"I have no doubt 'bout that, Mrs. Wells."

"So, Dusty, when is this big event going to happen?" Lisa inquired.

"Gosh, I don't know, Mrs. Wells. We have a few details yet to work out. But I hope it can be *real* soon."

"Well, one thing I know for sure," Lisa began, "it isn't going to happen until Clint returns. He would not want to miss your wedding."

"Oh, I completely agree, Lisa," Jenny said.

"Jenny, tomorrow, when I get home from school, we'll get my wedding dress out of storage and see if we can make some alterations so that it will fit you," Lisa announced.

"You would do that for me?" Jenny asked.

"Absolutely! Now, you *are* a couple of inches taller than me … and a bit larger 'bout the waist … but I think we can make it fit just fine," proclaimed Lisa, confidently.

Jenny began to sob. Dusty quickly wrapped his arms around her. Jenny's children, Maree and Kris, ran to their mother and put their arms around her, too. They now realized that Dusty was soon going to be their new father—and they couldn't be happier.

"Doggone if you don't have a way of git'n things done 'round here, Mrs. Wells," Charlie commented.

"Well, Mister Rhodes, I do hope you approve?" asked Lisa, not really requiring an answer to her question.

"By all means, ma'am! Now, why don't you get busy and find *me* a wife. I think after all these years of bein' alone it's high-time I got hitched."

"I think so, too, Mister Rhodes," declared Lisa, in total agreement. "I'll see what I can do 'bout your situation."

"Tomorrow," Dusty began, "we'll tell everyone over at Double Creek Ranch about our engagement. Perhaps Miss Lynne could contact her friend, Pastor Vargas, and ask him if he would be so kind as to marry us."

Chapter Eight

Thursday morning came much too quickly for the weary rangers. The sun was scarcely an hour above the eastern horizon when the rangers spurred their mounts northeast—with their prisoners leading the way. Carrizo Creek way station was their next planned watering hole.

The prisoners, so far, had not given the rangers any trouble since their departure from the canyon. Of the eleven raiders, only four were taken alive—and one of them, Tull Oaks, had a serious gunshot wound in his thigh. There was a slim possibility he could die from shock or infection before reaching Show Low. It was often ballyhooed by outlaws that dying from a gunshot was generally preferred over hanging, or doing a lifetime stretch inside Yuma's notorious prison.

Around ten o'clock, the rangers rode up in front of the Carrizo Creek way station. They decided to go ahead and have an early lunch. In a short while, they would be saying goodbye to Walt Eagar. He would be riding eastward to Fort Apache—carrying with him the distressing news about Jess McCain. Ranger Eagar was dreading telling Buck McCain about the death of his younger brother.

It was nearly eleven o'clock when Ranger Eagar mounted up and reined his mare toward Fort Apache. Before him was twenty-six lonely miles. The journey had been a lot more enjoyable on Tuesday when he had been riding in the company of his friend, Jess McCain.

"Men, let's get moving toward Show Low," Williamson ordered. "We've got nearly five hours of trail ahead of us. We ought to make it there by supper time."

The rangers were about twenty minutes north of Carrizo Creek when Tull Oaks toppled from his horse. Clint quickly dismounted and ran over to check on his condition. He was delirious and sweating profusely. Clint checked the wound on the raider's leg and noticed that it was oozing blood.

"Got a problem, Tom! He's bleeding … and burning up with fever! Not sure he's gonna make it to Show Low!"

"It's for sure he won't be forking a saddle anymore today. We've got to rig up something," Williamson said.

"I've got an idea," Clint quickly responded.

It took nearly an hour to assemble a *travois* (a primitive sledge) using the trunks from a couple of small four-inch diameter trees. Two bedrolls were tied between the poles—forming a cot-like bed. A pole was then secured to each stirrup of Oaks' saddle. His horse would now be dragging him all the way to Show Low—in the same manner that Plains Indians transported their belongings from place to place.

"Do ya think it will work, Clint?" Jim asked.

"It should work fine, Jim. But it will certainly tire out his horse a lot quicker. It's just too bad we don't have some sort of wagon. It would make transporting him a lot easier."

Two hours later, the group arrived at Juniper Woods way station. At least five inches on the tip of each pole of the *travois* had been shaved away by the roadway's hard surface.

"Do ya think those poles will last till we get to Show Low?" inquired Will, as he scratched at the side of his neck.

"Not a problem, Will!" Clint shot back.

Williamson dismounted and gave a new directive, saying: "Will, let's get Oaks out of the sun. Jim, I'd like for you to water our horses

… and Clint, you watch the prisoners."

"Can do, Captain," Jim replied.

With the assistance of Will Clowers, Williamson carried Tull Oaks inside the way station. Oaks appeared to be in a semi-conscious state. Will checked the wound. It was greatly inflamed and still oozing blood.

"We've got to get this wound cleaned out again. I think it's done gone septic on us, Captain," Will surmised.

The station manager heated up a pan of water, rounded up some clean rags, and produced a bottle of whiskey he had stashed in the back room.

Will and the station manager carefully cleaned out the wound. They finished by tightly wrapping Oaks' thigh with some clean bandages.

"That's all we can do for him now. His fever is still raging. He needs a doctor … and soon," Will reported.

Williamson turned to the station manager and asked: "How far to Show Low from here?"

"Oh, I reckon it's not more 'n sixteen miles. But, ya'd be hard pressed to arrive there by dark … especially with this here sick prisoner slowin' ya down."

"I'm guessing you're right in what you say," agreed Williamson, with a heavy sigh. "If you have no objections, sir, we'll bivouac here tonight."

"Reckon I don't. Be more 'n glad for the company. Ever since the stagecoach and freight wagons stopped running by here … well, it's been rather lonely 'round these parts."

"Well, sir, that situation should be changing for you real soon. Because the *raiders of Salt River Canyon* are no longer a threat to anyone along this route," explained Williamson, with an air of satisfaction.

"I'm glad to hear that!" commended the manager.

"Will, please inform Clint and Jim that we're hunkering down here for the night. And give 'em a hand."

"Sure thing, Captain," replied Will, as he scurried out the door. He found his fellow rangers at the corral.

While the station manager and Williamson looked after Oaks,

the rest of the rangers stripped the riding horses and packhorses of their saddles and "sawbuck" packsaddles, respectively. All the horses were soon turned out into the empty corral. There was some hay stored nearby under a large, makeshift lean-to. A quick investigation showed it to be free of mold. The rangers hauled several bales to the corral and scattered them about. The horses nearly knocked each other down getting to it. Liberty and Blanco bumped their way to the head of the line. None of the other horses protested.

Cal Amarē, Aikey Hart and Forrest Woods were secured to a hefty support post beneath the lean-to. Jim volunteered to keep a close eye on them while Clint and Will prepared the campsite.

As the sun was setting, Captain Williamson came out onto the porch to see how things were going. He was pleased at the progress. "Lookin' good, gentlemen!"

"Thanks, Tom!" Clint yelled from the nearby corral. He was now busy currying Liberty. Clint always made sure that his stallion was well cared for. He could not neglect a horse as fine as this one. Liberty had been his "bread and butter" when it came to launching his horse breeding operation.

Liberty, a liver-colored chestnut with superb conformation, stood better than sixteen hands. What set him off was the large white blaze on his forehead and the four closely matching white stockings. He had a wonderful disposition—despite the breeds' tendency to be high-strung and temperamental. And, like most Thoroughbreds, he had great stamina.

Williamson realized that he, too, needed to get busy and see to the needs of his gelding, Blanco. He hated it that he hadn't given his animal the proper attention it required. He vowed to treat his horse to the very best that the local livery could provide when they got to Show Low.

Seeing that there was nothing he could accomplish outside at the moment, he re-entered the way station and checked again on the wounded raider.

"He don't look so good," the manager noted.

"No, he certainly doesn't," Williamson readily agreed.

"He might be goin' into shock," the manager guessed. "That leg bone is shore busted up somethin' awful."

"I don't think he'll be leaving here in the morning," surmised Williamson, with a slight sigh.

"Yeah. Reckon I ought to go out to the shed and look for that ol' rusty shovel of mine," the manager concluded.

"Sir, I failed to get your name the last time we rode through here. On that day, we were in a hurry to get to the canyon and take care of business," Williamson said, as he extended his hand in friendship.

"I'm Ned Chance. Folks 'round here call me Slim. And your handle would be—"

"Williamson—Tom Williamson. Just call me Tom."

"Do you normally work out of these parts, Tom?"

"No. My men and I are headquartered at Fort Verde. But we are responsible for a wide area."

"Is this your whole company?"

"No. I have two other full-time men. They had other obligations this week. I also have a couple of reservist. One of them is with me on this trip. His name is Wells.

"Sounds to me like you could use a lot more men."

"You are right about that, Slim. I lost two men a couple of years ago up on the Mogollon Rim. Sadly, we lost another man on this mission. He was assigned to Fort Apache."

"Sorry to hear about your loss, Tom."

Williamson and the station manager conversed back and forth well into the evening. Slim had been spellbound as he listened to the ranger's telling of the sortie on the *raiders of Salt River Canyon.*

Williamson suddenly realized he had wholly lost track of the time. He jumped to his feet and walked to the door.

"If you don't mind, Slim," Williamson began, "I want to bunk in here tonight so I can keep a close eye on this wounded prisoner."

"You'll get no hassle from me. I've got a cot in the back room. I'll go fetch it fer ya."

"Sounds good," replied Williamson, as he glanced at his pocket watch. It was nine o'clock. I'll be back in a minute. Got to let my rangers know what's going on here."

Williamson went outside and talked briefly with Clint, Will and Jim. He disclosed the arrangements for their overnight stay at the way station, including their equal division of the guard duty. Each man would complete a four-hour shift.

With a campfire illuminating the now dark sky, Clint took the first watch. He couldn't sleep anyway. His thoughts were on Lisa and Lena. He missed them more than words could say. With a little luck, he hoped to be home with them by the end of the week.

Clint thought back over all the lonely years he spent wearing the badge of a Texas Ranger. During those years, he refused to entertain any thoughts of having a family as long as he was wearing a badge. That mind-set changed after he surrendered his badge, moved to central Arizona, and met a remarkable woman by the name of Lisa Reavis.

But, even before he met Lisa, Captain Williamson (a sergeant at the time) had sought him out and convinced him to join the Arizona Rangers. He only agreed to the job as long as it remained a temporary assignment. So far, the leader of the local band of rangers had kept his promise. For the past two and a half years, this was only his fifth outing with Williamson and the rest of the rangers.

Clint remembered how upsetting it had been to Lisa when he disclosed the fact that he had agreed to join the rangers. They were just dating at that time. She had been more understanding back then. But now that they were married and had a thirteen-month-old baby girl—well, things were different with her. She got more and more testy every time Williamson showed up at their door. *I'm so glad most of his visits were of a social nature*, he murmured to himself.

Suddenly, a loud groan and the sound of someone running off into the darkness interrupted Clint's thoughts. He sprang to his feet and ran to the lean-to where the three prisoners had been tied to a support post.

When he arrived at the lean-to, he found Forrest Woods bleeding profusely from a knife wound to the chest. He appeared to be dead. Cal Amarē and Aikey Hart were gone.

Clint could not believe his luck. Had he been so deep in his thoughts that he permitted their escape? Or was it possible he had momentarily fallen asleep? He wasn't sure.

Though anxious to track the escapees, he realized that there was no point in running off into the dark looking for them. It would be nothing short of committing suicide. He decided to alert his comrades first. They were sleeping just ten yards away—near the corral. He hadn't ventured a dozen steps when he heard a gasping sound; and faint, garbled words coming from Woods.

He's not dead! Oh, thank goodness, Clint muttered to himself. He immediately knelt down to see if he could make sense of what Woods was saying to him.

"Th-they got me ba-back for rat'n (choke) on them. Cal (gasp) ha-had a knife in his boot. Cut (cough) the ro-ropes and sta-stabbed (cough) me."

"Hang on, I'll get some help for ya."

Clint leaped to his feet and ran to Will and Jim. He woke them up and related to them what had just happened. They immediately stood watch over the horses in case the two escapees tried to steal a couple of them.

Clint entered the way station to wake the captain, but the man was already crouched behind a chair with his gun drawn—and leveled at the door. Clint was glad that his friend did not fire his six-shooter before he identified himself.

"It's me, Tom! Clint! We've got a major problem!"

"What's going on, Clint? I heard a ruckus outside."

"I'm so sorry, Tom, but two of our prisoners got away. I didn't hear a darn thing until it was too late. Woods has been stabbed. He claimed it was payback for rat'n on his pards. It seems Amarē had a knife tucked away in his boot."

"Don't worry about it, Clint. We can't do a thing tonight except keep our eyes peeled. They may try to sneak back in here and steal a couple of horses."

"Jim and Will are awake and guarding the horses. I think the knife wound in Woods' chest is fatal. It's very close to his heart. Reckon I'd best get back to the lean-to and see if there's anything I can do for him."

"I'll go with you. It looks like Oaks is still in a bad way. He may not make it through the night."

Clint, accompanied by Captain Williamson, rushed to the lean-to. When they got there, Woods was silent. Clint felt his neck for any sign of a heartbeat—none was detected.

"He's done for, Tom,"—Clint sighed heavily—"and it's all my

fault."

"No, Clint, it's not. We've been working with the bare minimum of men on this job. We're all tired, sleepy, and mentally worn out. All we can do now is just dig down deeper and draw on whatever reserve energy we have remaining."

Jim and Will joined Clint and Williamson at the lean-to. A blind man could easily see how exhausted they all were.

"Is he dead?" Jim asked.

"I'm afraid so," confirmed Clint, with a bit of sadness in his voice. "It should not have happened."

"Clint, these men had choices in life," Williamson began, "and they could have done something good with the life God gave them … but they chose evil. Sin has consequences, and they are finding that out the hard way. I think the Good Book says, 'He who lives by the sword—shall die by the sword.'"

"I know, but—"

"Let it go, Clint!" Williamson said, firmly. "We'll go after them two fugitives at first light. They surely can't get too far in the dark … and on foot."

Williamson turned and addressed Will and Jim, saying: "You two need to get back into your bedrolls. Clint will keep watch on things out here until his shift is over.

"It's ten o'clock now … so in two hours one of you will relieve him. Considering the present circumstances, we'll be breaking camp in the morning a lot earlier than we had originally planned." Williamson paused for a moment, and then asked: "Any questions?"

No questions were voiced.

"Okay, then. Get some rest," Williamson concluded.

Jim and Will retired to their bedrolls. Clint went back to the campfire and piled on some more wood to increase the light around the corral. With that done, he took up a position in the dark—with a clear view of the corral.

The next two hours seemed to creep by at a snail's pace. Midnight finally came. It was time to wake Jim.

Clint crawled into his bedroll. He was so upset with himself that it took him nearly an hour to fall asleep. But sleep did come at last to his tired, aching body.

Tomorrow would be a new day—a day of reckoning.

Chapter Nine

Friday morning. The first sunrays of the new day brought more bad news. Sometime during the night, Tull Oaks succumbed to shock and a gangrenous infection. The poison most likely attacked his heart.

The rangers "burned" the first hour of daylight burying Woods and Oaks in shallow graves they had dug behind the storage shed. They used up an additional thirty minutes searching a wide area around the way station looking for boot tracks.

"Over here!" Jim yelled out.

The tracks led the rangers north approximately two hundred yards, and then eastward a hundred yards to the stage road, and finally toward the northeast.

"The signs are clear to me. I think we all know where they are headed. Show Low!" Clint surmised.

"Let's round up our horses and gear and get after them slippery *varmints*," Williamson ordered.

It was roughly sixteen miles to Show Low. Factoring in the fugitives' head start of ten hours, it was very likely they had made it to Show Low before sunrise. With the near full moon that had lit the night sky, they would have had a somewhat clear view of the road.

By eight o'clock, the rangers had everything packed and were ready to travel. Since the horses were well rested, they planned to push them as hard as possible in hopes of catching up to the two fugitives before they had a chance to inflict havoc on Show Low's unsuspecting citizens.

The rangers thanked Slim for his hospitality, mounted their horses, and lit out for Show Low. They left the raiders' four horses at the way station.

"Once Amarē and Hart reach Show Low, they will most likely steal a couple of horses," Clint surmised.

"I have no doubt of that," Williamson agreed.

"If you want, Tom, I can push Liberty on ahead of y'all and see if I can run them two *coyotes* down."

"No, Clint. I'd rather we stay together. I know that horse of yours could beat us there by thirty minutes or more, but I would feel better knowing we remained unified."

Two hours later, the rangers stopped on the outskirts of Show Low. The boot tracks had never strayed far from the roadway. It was obvious that the raiders had made it to town ahead of them. The rangers also realized that the two raiders could be hiding somewhere in the town with some newly acquired guns, primed and waiting for them to ride into view.

"Stay alert, men … and spread yourselves out some," Williamson commanded. "There's no telling where they are. We're an easy target if we stay bunched up."

As they rode into town, Clint was the first to spot a small group of men standing in front of the sheriff's office. He hastily rode in that direction. Williamson, Will and Jim remained close behind. Each ranger was carefully scouting both sides of the street for anyone looking to ambush them.

As Clint got closer, it was clear that two of the men talking to the sheriff were very upset. One man was waving his arms in the air and cursing a blue streak.

"Now, Duffy, calm down! I'll find that roan of yours," Sheriff Hannagan promised.

"Well, what about my horse, Sheriff?" shouted the second man, just as irate as the first.

"That goes for yore sorry nag, too, Shorty!" Hannagan loudly proclaimed above the din of the crowd.

Williamson, Will and Jim joined Clint at the hitching rail near the sheriff's office. They all dismounted and walked over to where Hannagan was trying to quiet the crowd. At that moment, Hannagan espied the rangers approaching him.

"Good morning, gentlemen! Would ya happen to be after a couple of horse thieves?"

"Yes, Ken, we could be at that! They escaped our custody last night," Williamson admitted.

"Sorry to hear that," replied Hannagan, sincerely.

Williamson continued, saying: "As far as we can tell, they walked nearly sixteen miles from Juniper Woods. They were unquestionably in need of some fresh mounts."

"I hope horses are all they got their hands on," Jim sighed. "We're tired of being shot at by those two *yahoos*."

Just then an elderly man came running up the street shouting at the top of his lungs. "Sheriff, I've been robbed!"

It was the local gunsmith. Though nearly out of breath, he still managed to report that his business had been broken into, and several new guns were missing—plus four boxes of ammunition.

"Looks like our greatest fear has come true," Jim grumbled. "What's next, Captain?"

"My guess is that they didn't hang around Show Low too long. We've got to put our heads together and come up with a workable plan … and fast. Meanwhile, let's get our horses over to the livery. They all need feed and water."

"It would certainly be nice if *we* could get fed and watered sometime today," said Will, expressing some frustration.

"Will, you're absolutely right," Williamson wholeheartedly agreed. "Reckon an army doesn't travel too far on an empty stomach."

"Ken," Williamson began, "will you join us at the Blue Moon Café? We could use your input."

"Sure thing, Tom. I'll join you as soon as I disperse this crowd and complete these robbery reports."

The rangers dropped off their tired mounts and packhorses at the livery. The stable worker promised to take good care of them. He said he would have them ready to travel again in about an hour.

Williamson and his men adjourned to the café. It wasn't long before Sheriff Ken Hannagan joined them. They all sat at a long table in the back of the room.

"Ken, in which direction do you feel like they've taken?" Williamson inquired of the veteran lawman.

"Not sure, Tom. Could have gone east to New Mexico, or north to Snowflake, or maybe west to Payson. There's one sure-fire way to find out."

"What way is that?" Williamson wanted to know.

"Send one of your men in each direction. Stop at the first way station you come to and inquire if the fugitives stopped to water their stolen mounts. It's the only idea I got at the moment," Hannagan admitted.

"I don't see how we could come up with anything better than that," Williamson confessed.

The lawmen promptly consumed their breakfast of steak and eggs, and "high-tailed" it to the livery. Their horses were ready to travel—as promised.

"Leave the packhorses here. They'll only slow you down. Will, ride east … Jim, head north … Clint, you go west," Williamson commanded. "I'll stay here and get messages wired to Holbrook, Springerville and Payson … alerting the various town marshals about our fugitives."

Williamson estimated it would take approximately two hours for each man to ride to his assigned way station, talk to any witnesses, and ride back to Show Low. He prayed that Hannagan's idea would pan out.

* * * * *

"What ya so down-in-the-mouth 'bout Aikey?"

"Ah, Cal—it's just—well, I kinda wish ol' Woody didn't have to die. But I realize he *was* a lowdown rat."

"Well, Aikey, he won't be rat'n us out again!" boasted Amarē, displaying fulfillment over killing one of his own men.

"Cal, I never knew that ya carried a folding knife in yore boot. That was purty smart."

"Well, my friend, ya do now. And ya'd be wise to do the same thing. It's gotten me out of more than one scrape."

"Cal, do you think our ol' pard, Tull, lived through the night? He was feelin' mighty poorly."

"Ain't no tell'n … but I'm guessin' he didn't. When he toppled off his horse … I knew then that he was a goner."

"Yeah. Well, that's too bad. He was a good man. Didn't ya think so, Cal?"

Amarē refrained from commenting.

"Speakin' of bein' hurt, how's that ankle doin'? It's a darn wonder, Aikey, that ya didn't bust a bone."

Amarē was referring to Hart's severely sprained ankle. While fleeing *on foot* to Show Low during the night, Hart had walked too close to the edge of the road and stepped into a large hole. He went down hard—violently twisting his ankle.

It took the better part of an hour before he could even put pressure on the joint. With twelve miles left to travel, Amarē didn't know if he should abandon his partner or assist him in walking. Lucky for Hart that Amarē picked the latter option. Something that Hart was most grateful for.

"It still hurts … a lot. But at least some of the swelling is going away," Hart reported. "I'm really glad, Cal, that ya stuck with me last night."

Again, Amarē refrained from commenting.

The raiders were now about fifteen miles out of Show Low. Had it not been for taking considerable time out to eat breakfast at the last way station, they could have put even more miles under their saddles.

"Are we git'n out of Arizona, Cal?"

"Yeah. I think we had best do that. Things are too hot 'round here since the inception of them rangers. They're a lot more determined than most *local* lawmen. Once they get on yore trail, they don't stop until yore in jail … or dead."

* * * * *

After forty-five minutes of riding east, Will Clowers arrived at the Silver Creek way station. In minutes, he had his answer. The two fugitives had not stopped there. After a brief rest, he headed west—back to Show Low.

It took nearly an hour for Jim O'Bryan to reach the Shumway way station. His inquiry concerning the two fugitives brought a negative reply as well. After a brief rest, he headed south—back to Show Low.

Forty minutes had elapsed by the time Clint Wells dismounted his horse in front of the Pinedale way station. The station manager was sitting on the front porch. Clint immediately apprised him of the reason for his visit. The manager confirmed that two men, fitting Amarē's and Hart's description, had recently been there.

"Ranger, they've got at least a ninety-minute head start on you," added the manager.

At that moment, a traveler exited the building and walked to his horse. Clint quickly approached him.

"Say, mister, are you headin' east or west?"

"East … to Show Low. Why ya asking?"

"Will you do me a big favor?"

"Well, that depends. What do you need?"

"I'm trackin' two hardcore killers, and I need you to stop at the sheriff's office in Show Low and inform Captain Williamson that our fugitives are headin' for Payson."

"I reckon I can do that," the traveler replied, but not sounding too enthusiastic.

"If ya hurry … I'll see to it that you get a part of the reward money. These *varmints* are dangerous, and the reward will be substantial. Just leave your name with the sheriff. Someone will be in touch with you."

"Say, lawman, you've got yourself a deal!"

"By the way, what's your name?"

"Lightman—Bud Lightman."

"Hurry, Bud! There's no time to waste!"

The man was mounted and riding east before Clint could say another word.

Clint watered his horse, mounted up, and bade farewell to the station manager. In seconds, he was out of sight. Clint didn't even take the time to give Liberty a proper rest. He couldn't—because his family and friends were directly in the path of Cal Amarē and Aikey Hart. And men like them—escapees from the law—were extremely desperate. They would do whatever it took to further their agenda.

Clint prayed that Lightman would hustle back to Show Low. He wanted the help of his comrades, but realized that it would probably take them over two hours just to catch up with him. Waiting on his friends was not something he could afford to do.

If they are headed for Payson ... that puts Robert Lynne and his family ... and my family directly in their path! Clint thought to himself.

There was no time to lose. He had to pursue the outlaws with utmost haste.

* * * * *

Will Clowers and Jim O'Bryan rode into Show Low just minutes apart. They both headed directly for the sheriff's office, where they expected Captain Williamson to be waiting for them. And he was.

"Nothin' to the north," Jim reported.

"And nothin' to the east," echoed Will.

"Has Clint reported in yet, boss?" Jim asked.

"No, but it's still a little early yet. Let's give him a few more minutes. While we're waiting, why don't you two wander over to the livery and retrieve our packhorses and supplies."

Jim and Will hurried out of the office and made a beeline for the livery. They had not been gone ten minutes when a man rushed into the sheriff's office.

"Say, mister, are you Williamson?"

"Yes, sir, I am."

"Got an important message for you from one of your rangers over at the Pinedale way station."

"What did he say?"

"Says to hurry! The men you are after are on their way to Payson!"

"Much obliged, mister! Please, give your name to the sheriff ... and where you can be located."

"Your man said something about a *reward*," he added, before walking over to Hannagan's desk.

"I'll see to it that you don't go home empty-handed."

A big smile formed on Lightman's face. Williamson quickly looked him over. He couldn't decide if the man was an upright citizen or just greedy. He finally decided on the latter—guessing that coveting money was more important to this man than helping out a ranger in trouble. The man had done his *good deed* for the day and now he wanted to get *paid*.

Williamson rushed out the door. He spotted Jim and Will walking toward him with two packhorses in-tow. He hurried forward to meet them in the street.

"Them *owl hoots* are headed for Payson! We've got to bust our tails and catch up with Clint!"

"Catch up? You mean he rode in, and then left without us?" asked Jim, with a hint of acidity in his voice.

"No! No! It wasn't like that!" Williamson exclaimed.

"Well, where *did* you get the tip?" Will asked.

"From a civilian messenger. Clint was at the Pinedale way station when he dispatched the man to us," explained Williamson, now feeling somewhat apprehensive.

"Reckon I don't fault Clint for not riding back to Show Low. It's my guess that he has probably reached Deer Springs by now," Jim said.

"Yes. And he's definitely got a *big* lead on us," Williamson concluded.

"If we're gonna do some hard riding … then I guess we better return these packhorses to the livery. They'll just slow us down," Will rightly surmised.

"Say, boss, ain't Clint's family situated right in the path of them mangy *coyotes*?" asked Jim, with concern written all over his face.

"Yes, they are," Williamson quickly confirmed. "And they could all be in grave danger."

"So why are we standin' here jawin'? Let's stir up some trail dust!" Jim shouted.

Chapter Ten

"Cal, do ya think them rangers have figured out which direction we're headin'?" asked Aikey Hart, apprehensively.

"It's possible. But don't ya worry none 'bout that. I figure we're at least two hours ahead of them troublesome rangers. They won't catch up to us anytime soon."

"Ya shore are soundin' mighty confident that we won't be caught by them rangers."

"Yeah. Maybe I am at that. Ya see ... I'm bet'n them rangers are searchin' to the east. And ya know why?"

"Reckon I don't."

"Cause they'll be thinkin' we've headed to the New Mexico border ... seein' how it's a whole lot closer."

"I shore do hope yore right in what ya say."

"Aikey, ol' pard, have I *ever* been wrong?"

Hart did not respond to his question. He knew in his mind that his boss had been wrong on many occasions. Most recent case in point: His boss had insisted on the gang hiding out in Salt River Canyon. He had claimed with absolute certainty that no lawman or posse would dare venture into the canyon and challenge them—not even the Arizona Rangers.

That certainly didn't ring true. Now all my pards are dead, he muttered to himself.

"Did ya say somethin', Aikey?"

"Naw. You only heard my empty stomach growling. I'm git'n a bit hungry. We passed by that Deer Springs way station. It would be nice to stop at the next station and put some more grub in our bellies. What do ya say, Cal?"

"I don't see why not. It's too bad we didn't have time to rustle up some supplies in Show Low."

"Yeah. That would've been nice," Hart agreed.

"Git'n our hands on these here horses and six-shooters was a lot more important at the time," Amarē added.

"It's too bad there wasn't some better horse flesh to pick from this morning. This is about the most knuckleheaded beast I've ever ridden," Hart complained.

"Can't say much for this roan I'm ridin' either."

"Cal, I reckon we can buy a few of the supplies we need in the next town we come to. I got myself almost ten dollars. What ya got in yore pocket?"

"Oh, maybe twenty dollars. I'm not fer sure."

* * * * *

It was early afternoon when Clint rode up to the Deer Springs way station. His one and only question to the station manager revealed that his fugitives had not been there.

Clint had not seen any tracks departing from the main road since leaving the Pinedale station. Based on that observation, he reasoned that Amarē and Hart were now skipping way stations, but still heading west. He hoped that they were just ahead of him—and that he was closing in on them. Feeling somewhat confident that he was right, he decided to ride on to the next way station.

After watering his horse, Clint bade farewell to the station manager, and reined Liberty in the direction of the main road. He knew his stallion was getting tired, but he had to catch Amarē and

Hart before they reached his or Robert's ranch. Odds were, the fugitives would want fresh horses—and he had a whole corral full.

* * * * *

Captain Williamson, Jim O'Bryan and Will Clowers were making good time. They had elected to pass up the Pinedale way station and make their first stop at Deer Springs.

Williamson was worried that Clint would try to take on the two raiders alone. He knew the former Texas Ranger could fend for himself, but there was always the chance that something could go wrong. And besides, a man deeply concerned about the welfare of his family could get careless, and place himself in a situation that he normally would avoid.

"We'll check in at the Deer Springs way station and rest the horses. Hopefully, Clint is waiting there for us."

"And if he's not?" Will asked.

"We'll keep on riding west until we catch up to him. There's no doubt in my mind that he has that stallion parting the wind at full steam."

* * * * *

Cal Amarē and Aikey Hart casually finished up their meal at Aspen Meadow way station and rode west once again. For men on the lam, they seemed overly confident that they were now safely out of the reach of the law.

"Where is it we are headin' Cal?"

"There's a town up ahead that I visited a couple of years ago. It's called Payson. It's where I first met up with Ty and Woody. I told 'em *back then* to look me up sometime."

"I was wonderin' where ya had met 'em before."

"Well, now ya know. But there's more to the story. It turns out that Ty went and killed some loud-mouthed drunk at the local saloon. Next thing I know, he's knockin' at my front door, with Woody in-tow, lookin' fer a place to hide out."

"Is that so? He never mentioned that to anyone."

"He was probably afraid someone in the gang would kill him for the reward," Amarē said, followed by a snicker.

"Just how much was the reward?"

"Oh, last I heard, it was a *thousand* dollars."

"That's a nice lump sum of ol' money!"

"Yeah, Aikey. That it is. Reckon them rangers have stunted the future income of some lowly bounty hunter."

"How far is it to this here ol' town of Payson?"

"Well, I ain't fer certain … could be thirty miles … or maybe forty," Amarē guessed.

"We won't get there before dark … that's fer shore."

"Yeah. That's why we need to find someplace to hold up for the night. It would be nice if could find us a ranch along this road. We might even pick us up some fresh horses."

"Good. This blasted calf-kneed nag I'm currently straddlin' shore ain't gonna last much longer," Hart griped.

"We'll find somethin' better soon," Amarē concluded.

* * * * *

Clint Wells had no desire to stop at Aspen Meadow way station, but he had no choice. He had to be certain that he was still on the trail of the two raiders.

The station manager quickly confirmed that the fugitives had indeed been there. He also mentioned that they had lingered about the station for a good while after eating their meal, and didn't seem to be in any hurry to ride out.

Clint was elated that he was still on their trail. He also discovered that they were now less than an hour ahead of him. He had closed in on them by over thirty minutes.

"If a band of rangers show up … let 'em know that I was here. Okay?"

"Can do, Ranger Wells. I hope you nab them *coyotes*!"

Clint allowed Liberty a small amount of water before riding out. He wished he could rest his steed for a spell, but too many lives were in danger. He had to catch the raiders before they inflicted more harm on the good people of the territory.

* * * * *

Captain Williamson and his men halted their horses in front of the Deer Springs station. The manager informed them that their comrade had been there, but that he had not seen the two fugitives they were seeking.

After giving the horses a brief rest, Williamson and his men were back on the trail. They now had a fair idea as to how far Clint had come—and how far ahead of them he was.

"He's really making good time, men. We may be a while catching up with him," Williamson surmised.

"What ever it takes, Captain!" Jim remarked.

"And that goes for me too," echoed Will.

"Are we stoppin' at the next station?" Jim asked.

"No. We'll keep going till we get to the Rim View station," Williamson replied.

"Captain, that's a good ways off. I hope my mare can hold up that long," Will said, showing a lot of concern.

"Point taken. We'll do the best we can."

* * * * *

Cal Amarē and Aikey Hart passed up the Forest Lakes way station in order to make up lost time. It was mid-afternoon when they rode up to the Rim View way station and tied their mounts to the hitching rail. Their horses were well lathered and wholly exhausted. Both raiders were exhausted, too, and wanting to get out of the saddle for an extended period.

The station manager was sitting on the porch. He carefully sized up the two disheveled-looking men standing in front of him. Not sensing any danger, he warmly greeted them.

Amarē wasted no time in asking the manager what was foremost on his mind. "Mister, is there a ranch near by where a man could buy a good horse?"

"Sure thing. There's a ranch just beyond the Basin Flat way station that has some of the finest horseflesh in these parts. Can't go wrong, mister, buyin' one of dem mounts. Just look for a big ol' sign that reads … *Rim Shadow Ranch*."

"Sounds perfect. I 'preciate the information."

"Glad I could be of help," responded the manager. As he spoke, a dribble of dark brown saliva escaped from the corner of his mouth. He quickly turned his head and spit out a glob of tobacco juice. Using his shirtsleeve, he wiped his chin.

"We gonna try and make it there today, Cal?" asked Hart, wishing that his partner would quit for the day and find a place to camp.

"You bet we are! And we'd best be movin' on."

During their descent from the Rim View station to Basin Flat, both men couldn't help but be awed by the marvelous views to the south. They were nearly seven thousand feet above sea level. A man could see nearly seventy miles from the top of the Mogollon Rim—perhaps even more on a clear winter day.

"Wow! I thought the Salt River Canyon was purty, Cal, but these views are somethin' else."

"Yeah. Not too bad at that," Amarē agreed.

"Cal, can we take a short break? I'd love to sit over there on that big boulder and enjoy the scenery for a bit."

"Shore, why not. We ain't in that big of a hurry."

* * * * *

Clint Wells passed up the Forest Lakes way station and continued on to the Rim View station. When he arrived he learned that the two raiders had stopped briefly to water their horses. The most alarming news was that they were indeed looking for new mounts. The station manager apologized to Clint for telling the fugitives where they could find the best horses in the territory—the Rim Shadow Ranch.

Based on other information that he had gleaned from the station manager, Clint was now reasonably certain that Amarē and Hart were less than twenty minutes ahead of him. This revelation made him even more determined—if that were possible—to close the gap.

Clint watered his horse and allowed him to rest for several minutes. He checked Liberty's lower legs and hoofs for any problems, and found none. Thankfully, for Liberty's sake, the next few miles were downhill.

Looking skyward, Clint prayed: *Thank you, Lord, for this strong and dependable steed.*

As he had done previously at the other way stations, Clint

instructed the station manager to pass along whatever information he had to the rangers that were trailing him.

In a minute or less, Clint was at the edge of the Rim. Unlike Amarē and Hart, Clint scarcely took notice of the commanding views from atop the Rim as he began his descent to Basin Flat. At this moment in time he was totally focused on his mission—capturing the last two remaining raiders. The by-product: Prevent calamity from thrusting itself upon his family and friends.

But, there was a time—two years ago—when he spent long moments soaking up the awesome vistas. It had been during his first encounter with the Mogollon Rim high-country. That was then; things were so much different now. As lovely as the vistas were, this was certainly not an opportune time for a repeat observation.

* * * * *

Cal Amarē and Aikey Hart noticed a small weathered sign that read: DOUBLE CREEK RANCH. They immediately reined in their horses.

"Is this the place, Cal?"

"Naw. The station manager said the place is called Rim Shadow Ranch. He said it was just down the road from this one. This here place is just another ol' way station."

"Well, I hope it ain't much farther, cause I'm beat!"

"Ya ain't got no monopoly on that. Buck up, pard. Let's ride. It's gotta be just up the road a short piece."

A quarter-mile later—perhaps a little less—the raiders espied another sign that read: RIM SHADOW RANCH — QUALITY HORSES FOR SALE.

"Looks like we done found what we've been lookin' fer, Aikey. Let's check it out."

"We gonna ride in there normal, or sneaky-like?"

"Reckon we'll just ride in there like normal folks and pretend we are horse buyers. Course we got no money … but they don't know that," replied Amarē, with a chuckle.

"What if they don't want to give up a couple of them horses to the likes of us?"

"No problem," Amarē began, "we'll just kill 'em."

* * * * *

It was late afternoon when Lisa, Maree and Kris arrived home after a long day at school. The buggy's wheels had barely stopped turning when the children leaped down from the seat and ran into the house to find their mother.

Lisa was taking steps to unhitch the horse from the buggy when she heard riders coming up the lane. She eagerly hoped it might be Clint and the other rangers returning from their weeklong mission.

As the two riders came swiftly into view, she felt a pang of disappointment—followed by deep concern for her safety when she saw how scruffy the riders were. She knew instinctively that she must not exhibit fear by running for the safety that the house might offer. Being diminutive in physical stature, she would have to put up a strong front.

"How ya do, ma'am. Would ya be the boss lady around here?" asked Amarē, as his eyes scanned the property.

"My husband and I run this ranch," Lisa answered. "May I know your reason for being here?"

"Of course, ma'am. We're lookin' to trade our mounts for a couple of your quality horses," continued Amarē, with a conniving grin forming on his grimy face.

"Yeah! The best horse flesh ya got," Hart added.

"I'm so sorry, gentlemen, but we only *sell* horses at this ranch. You'll need to discuss *trading* your horses with my husband," Lisa explained.

"That'll be fine, ma'am. Where can we find this husband of yores?" asked Amarē, while continuing to survey the property. His right hand was now resting uneasily on the wooden handgrip of his stolen six-shooter.

"He's away on business, but I'm expecting him back any time now," Lisa fibbed, hoping that her statement would cause them to ride away in fear to avoid possible trouble.

"Ya don't say?" Amarē sourly fired back.

"Just leave your names and where you can be reached. My husband will gladly contact you. I'll go in the house and fetch a leaf of paper to write down your information."

As she started toward the house, Aikey Hart quickly reined his mount in front of her, blocking her pathway. When she tried to go around, he again blocked her pathway.

"What's the meaning of this?" Lisa demanded to know, as she looked toward the house to see if Jenny or any of the children were aware of what was going on. She saw no one.

"Ma'am, we need them horses, and we ain't gonna wait for yore man to get back from his errand. If yore real smart … ya won't get in our way," Amarē threatened.

When Hart swung his leg over the cantle to dismount, Lisa shoved his horse backward with all her might, and bolted for the house. Hart quickly jumped clear of his stumbling horse. Despite his sore, swollen ankle, he ran after her. Before she could ascend the porch steps, he grabbed hold of her arm and jerked her back against his own body. He quickly wrapped both his arms tightly around her slender body.

Lisa let out an ear-piercing scream as she tried to free herself by fiercely twisting her body in Hart's burly arms, but it was of no avail. She tried to scream again, but the man's big grimy hand quickly covered her mouth. Lisa hoped that Jenny had heard her first scream.

At that moment, Amarē raced up to the porch on his horse, dismounted, and rushed into the house. He knocked Jenny flat on her back just as she was reaching up for the carbine that was anchored to hooks just above the front door.

Jenny was momentarily stunned. After collecting her wits, Jenny yelled at the top of her voice to her two children, who were playing in the kitchen, saying: "Maree! Kris! Go fetch Robert! Hurry!"

As Amarē struggled to subdue her, the two older children dashed out the back door, leaving Lena all alone in the kitchen. The frightened little girl began to whimper.

Hart, meanwhile, had wrestled Lisa to the ground, and was tying her hands behind her back with a strip of rawhide. "Good grief, Cal, this redhead is a real fighter!" he yelled out.

"Get her under control, and bring her in the house!" Amarē ordered. "We gotta grab them fresh horses and get outta here before them brats come back with help!"

In less than a minute, Lisa was forced into the house, and swiftly tied back-to-back with Jenny in two of the kitchen chairs. Both were then gagged.

Fearing the circumstances around her, little Lena was now crying at the top of her lungs. She made her way to her mother, and clung tightly to her legs.

"What are we gonna do with this kid?" Hart asked.

"We'll take her with us … just in case someone shows up before we can get dem horses saddled and ride out of here."

Amarē rushed out the door with little Lena tucked under his left arm. The child was still bawling her head off.

Hart rounded up the two depleted horses and began unsaddling them as fast as he could. Amarē, meanwhile, picked out two fresh horses from the corral and herded them toward Hart. "Take these two, Aikey! Git 'em saddled … and hurry!"

* * * * *

Williamson and his men passed up the Aspen Meadow way station, but were forced to stop at the Forest Lakes station. Their horses, now wholly exhausted, needed a short rest and some cool water.

When asked, the station manager reported that he had not seen Ranger Wells or the two fugitives that were described to him. This was a big disappointment to the rangers.

"Clint's probably riding straight for his ranch. He most likely has one thing on his mind right now … protecting his family," Williamson stated with uncertainty.

"I'm ready to go if y'all are," said Jim, with untiring determination written all over his face.

"Okay then … let's ride!" Williamson ordered.

Blanco reared slightly and sped down the lane to the main road. The mares that O'Bryan and Clowers were riding could only wish that they had that kind of energy.

Chapter Eleven

Clint Wells knew that he could not ride openly down the lane to his home. Instead, he rode directly to Robert's ranch. As he was dismounting in front of the house, he noticed Maree and Kris running out of the woods directly toward him.

"Uncle Clint! Uncle Clint! Help! Mama and Aunt Lisa are in big trouble! Ya gotta help 'em! Some really bad men are hurtin' 'em!" shouted Maree, while trying to catch her breath.

"I'm scared, Uncle Clint!" exclaimed Kris.

"Calm down, children. It will be okay. I'll take care of everything. You just stay here where it's safe."

"Oh, please, Uncle Clint … do hurry," begged Maree.

At that moment, Rebecca Lynne came rushing out of the house. "Clint! What's going on here? Are the children all right? Are you all right?"

"Two dangerous fugitives have accosted Lisa and Jenny. They are most likely trying to steal a couple of my horses. Is Robert here … or Charlie?"

"No, Clint. Robert rode over to Charlie's place nearly an hour ago. I'm not sure when he'll be back."

"What 'bout Dusty?" he asked.

"No. Dusty is with Charlie as far as I know," Rebecca surmised.

Just then, Connie Lynne came running up to where everyone was standing. "Clint! Welcome back!" Connie shouted enthusiastically. "I'm so happy tha—"

As a matter of urgency, Clint cut her off in mid-sentence. "Keep the children here," Clint commanded. "I've got to get to my ranch before it's too late. I'll cut through the woods … maybe they won't see me slippin' up on 'em."

"Clint, what's wrong?" asked Connie, her face reflecting deep concern.

"The children will have to fill you in. I've got to go!" Clint grabbed his carbine from his scabbard and lit out for the footpath that connected Robert's ranch with his.

As soon as Connie got the details from the children as to what was happening, she ran back to her house, grabbed her own carbine, and chased after Clint.

In minutes, Clint was positioned behind a large ponderosa pine where he could observe the two raiders without being detected. He cringed when he saw his little girl dangling from Cal Amarē's arm. He realized he could not put his daughter's life in danger by advancing on them. He just hoped the fugitive would put her down when he was ready to ride out.

Suddenly, Clint heard something behind him. He spun around expecting danger. It was Connie. "What are you doin' here?" he whispered.

"Helping you, that's what," she replied in a low voice, as she crouched down next to him. "And don't even entertain the thought of sending me away."

"I wouldn't think of it."

"Have you seen Lisa and Jenny?"

"No. I'm guessing they are in the house."

"Clint, just who *are* these men?"

"They *were* my prisoners. I'm responsible for them being here. If I had been watching them properly, they would be in jail right now," explained Clint, forlornly.

"I don't understand, Clint," Connie whispered.

"I'll explain it all later. Right now we need a plan to rescue little Lena. I gotta figure out a way to distract them."

"I just might have the solution," Connie replied.

And without saying another word, Connie stealthily walked north through the woods and then slightly west until she had the raiders in a crossfire situation. Once she was in place, she sucked in a deep breath, and walked out into the open courtyard with her carbine pointed directly at the fugitives.

"You two *polecats* stop what you're doing … and put that child down … or so help me … I'll plug you both!"

Clint realized what Connie was doing. She had focused their attention on her. They now had their backs to his position. Taking advantage of the situation, he stealthily slipped out of the woods, and made a beeline for the back door of his house. He spotted the women in the kitchen—bound and gagged.

Connie, meanwhile, continued to focus her carbine on the two raiders. "What's the matter … you mangy cowards need a little child to protect you from a woman?"

"Lady, unless ya want to see this brat die in front of yore purty eyes … I suggest you unhand that carbine," Amarē threatened, as he drew his stolen single-action revolver and aimed it directly at Lena's head.

"You wouldn't dare!" she screamed.

Amarē eased back the revolver's hammer while Connie watched in complete horror.

"Okay! Okay! You win!" she cried, as she eased the carbine's hammer forward and slowly lowered it to the ground. "Now, please, give me the child!"

"Gladly!" shouted Amarē, as he released the now squirming and screaming child. "And shut her up!"

Lena, still screaming out for her mother, started walking toward Connie as fast as her little legs could carry her. Unable to wait for her, Connie ran forward several steps and swept the child upward into her comforting arms. "You *skunks* ought to be ashamed of yourselves! You've scared this poor child nearly to death."

Amarē exploded, saying: "Shut yer blasted yap, lady … or I'll be obliged to shut it for you!"

"Burn in hell!" she fired back.

"Lady, yore not only purty … with them dark brown eyes and that long raven-colored hair … but sassy as well. I like a woman with yore spirit," he countered.

"Seein' how you two are git'n along so well … I shore hate to interrupt … but the horses are saddled and ready," reported Hart. "Now, let's git outta here, Cal … and *pronto*!"

"You know what, Aikey? It just occurred to me that there are no men folk around here. Why else would a woman show up here all alone to rescue her neighbors?"

"Who cares, Cal. Let's git!"

"Maybe we should have us a little fun first. This is one fine lookin' gal we got here. She shore does fill out a dress in a mighty fine fashion."

"No way! Come on! Let's git outta here!"

Hart's words of warning were falling on deaf ears.

* * * * *

Clint had made his way to Lisa and Jenny. His shaking hands made it difficult to untie the ropes, but with some effort, he finally released the knots.

Lisa jerked the rope away from her nimble body, ripped the gag from her mouth, and bolted for the front door before Clint could stop her. She could not reason beyond rescuing Lena from the horse thieves. It was something a devoted mother was bound in her heart to do.

"Lisa, wait! Don't go out there!" Clint shouted.

Amarē, hearing the screen door slam back against the porch wall, spun around and fired his six-shooter in one rapid uninterrupted motion at the lithe figure dashing down the front steps of the house. He had taken no time to discern if it was a man or a woman. The advancing figure folded over and tumbled to the ground.

Jenny screamed when she heard the gunshot, even though she couldn't see what had just taken place. Connie, who wholly witnessed the event, quickly dropped to her knees, still clutching tightly to Lena as she did. She instantly felt sick to her stomach.

Tears began to roll down her cheeks.

Another shot rang out! A fraction of a second later, Cal Amarē was grabbing his chest as a bullet from Clint's carbine tore through him. The leader of the notorious raiders glanced wide-eyed at his partner, spit up blood, and crashed to the earth. His life as an outlaw had come to a violent end.

Hart, now busy trying to control the horse he had just mounted, failed to see Connie reaching for her carbine. By the time he became aware of her threat, it was too late. Connie's carbine roared, further spooking the horse. It reared up, spilling Hart from the saddle. Not only was he stunned by the fall, but he also had a gaping hole in his left side. He slowly raised himself up, drew his revolver, and leveled it at Connie.

* * * * *

Captain Williamson and his men had stopped briefly at the Rim View way station. From the station manager they learned that not only had the fugitives been there, but Clint as well. The manager sadly admitted to the rangers that he had regrettably steered the raiders to Clint's ranch in their search for fresh horses.

The rangers had departed Rim View station in a cloud of dust. They passed up Basin Flat way station, and were now near enough to Clint's ranch that they could hear the gunfire, though quite faintly.

"Did you hear that?" Williamson asked his men.

"Gunfire!" Jim shouted.

"It's got to be comin' from Clint's place!" Will reasoned. "I hope we aren't too late to be of any help."

"I hope these horses have something left in them," Williamson said. "We've still got some distance to cover."

It was at least another mile to Clint's ranch. Williamson didn't know if his steed, Blanco, had anything left to give him, but he had to try and assist his friend—no matter the cost. He spurred his mount into a full gallop.

Blanco pulled far ahead of the horses being ridden by Will and Jim. Will spurred his mare, but she did not respond to his wishes. He finally coaxed her into a gentle lope. Jim's mare had a little more left in her, and she tried her best to catch up with Blanco. However, a hundred yards later, she gave out. Jim, too, reined his horse back into a lope.

In minutes, Captain Williamson was galloping down the lane to Clint's house. As the ranch house was coming into view, he heard another gunshot.

* * * * *

Aikey Hart would probably have died in a few hours from the bullet that Connie put through his kidney, but no one will ever know for certain—for her second shot hit him squarely between the eyes. He had underestimated her ability to handle a carbine.

As soon as she had dealt with the raider, Connie grabbed up Lena and raced toward the house where Lisa was being cradled in Clint's arms.

As Clint sat on the ground holding her, he could feel the life quickly fading from her body. Soon, he would lose his beautiful *little mountain girl*. Never again would he know her love, and experience the "free spirit" in her that made her so special to him. He began to sob.

Connie and Jenny stood over Clint and Lisa. Both were fighting back tears. Little Lena—secure in Connie's embrace—looked on, but not understanding the tragedy that had unfolded right before her eyes. Connie's heart was breaking for this little girl and her father. She wished there was something she could do, but she felt helpless.

Captain Williamson examined the two raiders, and found them to be deceased. *Justice has been served*, he thought. He now worried that Clint would forever blame himself for these men escaping from his custody, coming to his ranch, and ultimately fatally wounding his wife. He removed his hat, and walked over to where Clint was holding Lisa, but did not get too close. He, too, felt helpless.

A moment later, Will and Jim rode into the courtyard. They were stunned by what they saw. Both immediately dismounted, removed their hats, and joined their leader.

Rebecca Lynne (armed with a pistol), Helen Myers (armed with a double-barreled shotgun), and Jenny's two children arrived on the scene just as Clint was carrying Lisa's lifeless body into the house. They were altogether shocked by what they saw. The children became quite emotional and had to be calmed by their mother. Rebecca and Mrs. Myers followed Clint into the house.

Aware that some things needed to be done, Connie Lynne took immediate charge of the situation at hand. Perhaps, she thought, if everyone had something to do it would ease his or her emotional distress.

"Maree," Connie began, "please saddle up your pony and ride over to Charlie's place and fetch Robert back here."

"Yes, ma'am." Maree's face was flooded with tears as she dashed to the barn to saddle Cholla.

"Will," continued Connie, "would you and Jim get those ghastly bodies out of sight? And, also, if you wouldn't mind, please unsaddle the horses that those men tried to steal and put them back in the corral."

"Yes, ma'am. We'd be glad to do that," Will said.

"Ma'am, what would you have us do with them nags that they rode in on?" inquired Jim. "They were stolen from some folks over in Show Low."

"Well, I certainly don't want them near the good stock. Just tie them over by the bunkhouse."

"Yes, ma'am."

"Ma'am, is there anything you would like for me to do?" Williamson asked.

"Yes, there is. Stay close to Clint until Robert gets here. He may need a sturdy shoulder to lean on."

"You can count on me, ma'am. I'll do just that." Having agreed to that, he hustled into the house to be with Clint.

Connie walked over to where Jenny and Kris were standing. They seemed lost in their grief. She put her arms around the boy's shoulders. "Kris, how would you like to do something very important for me?" she asked.

"Wha-what would that be, Miss Lynne?" he asked, as he wiped the tears away from his face with his shirtsleeve.

"Do you think you could finish unhitching Lisa's horse from the buggy and get him watered and fed?"

"Yes, ma'am," he answered, while wiping his face one more time to clear the next wave of tears.

"Jenny, you and I had probably go in the house and see if there is anything we can do to assist Rebecca and Aunt Helen. I don't see much else to be done out here."

"Oh, Connie, I feel so bad for Clint and little Lena."

"I certainly feel the same. However, we must be strong for them. And most importantly, we must *pray* for them."

"Yes, Connie, you're so right," Jenny agreed. "Only God can truly comfort them in such a dreadful situation as this," she added.

* * * * *

Twenty minutes had elapsed by the time Maree returned with Robert. Charlie and Dusty were with her as well.

When Robert walked into the house, he saw Clint standing over Lisa. She was lying on a blanket atop the kitchen table. A sheet had been placed over her body, but not her face.

Robert walked over to Clint and put his arm around his friend's shoulder. Clint began to sob once more. In seconds, Robert was sobbing too. Charlie and Dusty stood nearby. Tears began running down their faces as well.

Mrs. Myers peered out the screen door and saw that the bodies of the raiders had been removed from the courtyard. She then approached Robert and requested that he take Clint outside while she and the ladies tended to Lisa.

Williamson, Charlie and Dusty joined Clint and Robert on the porch. Each one expressed his deepest condolences to Clint. As he sat back in one of the rocking chairs, Clint thanked them, but said little more. He was obviously *cut to the heart* by Lisa's death.

Charlie and Dusty excused themselves and went to the aid of Jim and Will. In record time, they had all the rangers' horses rubbed down, watered, and fed. Even the two nags stolen in Show Low were cared for—but not placed in the corral. Jim returned them to the hitching rail in front of the bunkhouse.

Speaking to Jim and Will, Charlie asked: "Where did ya hide dem bodies?"

"We rolled 'em in canvas and put 'em inside the tool shed to keep the critters from chewin' on 'em," Jim replied.

"Well, furst thang in the mornin' I'll haul dem bodies off to

Payson and let Marshal Chandler have the pleasure of buryin' 'em," declared Charlie. "And I'll take along dem scruffy nags they rode in on, too."

Charlie figured that the horses' owners could commute by stagecoach to Payson and pick them up. He would have Marshal Chandler send a wire to Sheriff Hannagan as to the whereabouts of the horses. He would also include a brief account of the events surrounding the demise of the raiders, and sadly, he would also disclose the death of Lisa Wells.

Just thinking about the latter caused Charlie's eyes to well up with tears.

When everyone had completed his or her assigned task, they congregated back at the house to ask Connie if anything else needed to be done. She had her short list ready.

Charlie Rhodes volunteered to build the coffin. Dusty said he would help his father. Williamson, O'Bryan and Clowers said they would dig the grave in the morning if someone would point out the location. And lastly, the women agreed to care for the children and finish preparing Lisa's body for burial.

"I guess that's all then," Connie concluded.

Captain Williamson was walking toward the corral to check on his horse when he heard footsteps running up behind him. It was Connie.

"Tom," she began, "I'll speak with Clint this evening and see if he has a particular place in mind for Lisa's grave."

"That would be fine, Miss Lynne."

"I'll let you know in the morning. Okay?"

"Yes, ma'am. I'll see ya then."

Clint did not spend the night at his ranch. Robert had convinced him to stay at the Double Creek Ranch. The children went along as well, and were placed in the care of Rebecca. Helen Myers returned to her home around mid-night. Rangers Williamson, O'Bryan and Clowers spent the night in Clint's bunkhouse. Connie and Jenny remained in the ranch house; neither woman wishing to leave Lisa's body unattended.

* * * * *

Before retiring, the rangers sat out on the porch of the bunkhouse and discussed the day's events. All three were deeply concerned for Clint. After a while the conversation turned to the disposition of the packhorses and the supplies that they had left behind in Show Low.

"Captain, do ya want me and Jim to return to Show Low tomorrow for dem packhorses?" Will asked.

"No. I'll send a wire to Sheriff Hannagan requesting that he sell the packhorses and packsaddles back to the owner of the livery stable. As for the food supplies … he can use them to feed any prisoners he may have in his jail."

"That makes sense to me," Jim responded.

"Yeah. I'll go along with that," Will echoed.

"Reckon we had best turn in, men," Williamson began, "cause we got a lot going on around here tomorrow."

* * * * *

Working feverishly into the night, Charlie Rhodes and his son, Dusty, prepared a cedar coffin for Lisa's body. When they were done, they loaded it onto the buckboard. They planned to deliver it to the Rim Shadow Ranch at first light.

"Do ya think Mr. Wells will like the coffin?" Dusty asked his father.

"Son, I don't think ya need to worry none 'bout that. He'll know that ya poured yore heart into buildin' it."

Dusty placed his hand on the coffin, sighed, and then said: "I just want Clint to be pleased with it."

"I know, son. Now, let's get cleaned up and call it a day. We've got to rise early. I'm sure that the ladies will do their part in getting the inside of it lined with all sorts of soft and frilly things," Charlie concluded.

Charlie put his arm around his son's shoulder and escorted him into the house. Tomorrow would be a very trying day for all concerned.

Chapter Twelve

Saturday morning came with a promise of hope for the future, but no one welcomed it. This would be the day that Lisa Wells would be laid to rest.

The sun was scarcely up when Charlie and Dusty arrived at the Rim Shadow Ranch. They carried the cedar coffin into the house and placed it in the living room on top of a pair of sturdy sawhorses. Its strong aromatic aroma quickly dispersed the aroma of the coffee that Connie and Jenny had just prepared for themselves.

"Oh, what a beautiful coffin … and it smells so heavenly. You did a wonderful job," remarked Jenny.

"Charlie … Dusty," Connie began, "would you like to join us for coffee?"

"We'd like that just fine, Miss Lynne," Charlie replied.

Dusty walked up to Jenny and put his arms around her and kissed her gently on the forehead. He could tell that she had not slept well. Her eyes were red and slightly swollen.

Connie filled two mugs with coffee and served them to the two sullen-looking men. After a few minutes of solemn conversation, the ladies busied themselves by decorating the coffin's interior. As soon as they were finished, Charlie and Dusty placed Lisa's body inside. Burial would be later that afternoon.

Charlie regretted that he would not be present for the burial, but he had to make that special trip to Payson. He didn't want Clint to come home and learn that the bodies of Cal Amarē and Aikey Hart were still on his property.

"Well, Miss Lynne," Charlie began, "reckon Dusty and I will load the corpses of them *coyotes* on the buckboard and round up dem nags. I want to get started for Payson."

"I understand. And thank you, Charlie, for all you and Dusty have done. The coffin is quite nice," Connie replied.

"Yes, ma'am. More 'n glad to be of service."

"Dusty, will you be going with your father?" asked Jenny; rather hoping he would stay with her.

"No. I'll not leave here. I want to help y'all."

Charlie and Dusty had not been gone but a few minutes when there came a knock at the door. Jenny went to the door to see who it was. It turned out to be the three rangers.

"Good morning. Please come in," she said.

"Thank you, ma'am," Williamson replied.

As they entered the house their focus went instantly to the new coffin. Jim was the first to walk over and peer inside.

"She looks like a sleepin' angel," he said.

Will quickly walked over and joined his friend. He looked down at the once lively form in the coffin. He started to say something, but words escaped him.

Ranger Williamson stood near the screen door, twisting his hat in his hands. Connie could tell he was emotionally shaken. She decided to come to his rescue. She walked over and grabbed his arm.

"Would you care for some coffee?" she asked.

"Tha-that would be nice, ma'am," he replied.

"I'll put on a fresh pot. Won't be a minute. Come on in the kitchen and sit down," she directed. "Hey, I'm speaking to you two as well," she added, pointing at Will and Jim.

"Ma'am, if you don't mind, I'd would prefer to have my coffee on the front porch," Williamson said.

"Jim and I will do the same," echoed Will.

"Oh, yes. I perfectly understand. I'll be out with your coffee in a few minutes."

The rangers filled the rocking chairs on the front porch and watched as Charlie drove the buckboard up the lane with the wrapped bodies of Cal Amarē and Aikey Hart in the back. He was en route to Payson. In-tow were the two horses stolen from the owners in Show Low.

Dusty returned to the house and greeted the rangers. He joined them, filling the last remaining rocking chair.

Dusty sighed, and said: "It's gonna be a terrible day."

"Yes, you're right. I just can't believe Mrs. Wells is dead. Why did that *hombre* have to shoot her?" Jim asked.

"Dusty tried to explain, saying: "I don't think he really meant to. Connie said it was like some kind of uncontrollable reflex. He just spun around and fired—not realizing if it was a man or a woman he was shooting at."

As the conversation moved along, Dusty began to show a great deal of interest in the rangers' line of work. When Jenny heard his voice, she came to the screen door to inquire if he wanted any more coffee. She overheard Dusty asking about the rangers and what qualifications were needed to join.

Jenny stormed out the door. "Oh, no, you don't!" she exclaimed. "You get them ideas out of your head, Mister Rhodes! My future husband isn't going to keep me up at nights wondering if he is dead or alive."

"I was *only* asking," Dusty countered.

Jenny gave Dusty a hard look and went back into the house. She told Connie what had just transpired. Tears were welling up in her eyes. Connie did her best to comfort her.

"Don't worry, Jenny. He'll not join the rangers. For one thing, I'll see to it that Tom doesn't hire him."

Jenny sucked in a deep breath and let it out slowly. She felt somewhat better after hearing Connie's reply.

"Connie, should I fix breakfast for us all?" asked Jenny, desperately wanting to get her mind off of things.

"Yes! That would be grand," replied Connie, as she leaned forward and gave her a gentle hug.

At that moment, Dusty came inside and addressed Jenny, saying: "I just wanted to let you know that I've got to be at Robert's before ten o'clock to assist with the stagecoach arriving from Payson. As soon as I get the team swapped around, I'll hurry back over here."

"That's fine," she answered sourly.

"Are you mad at me?" he asked.

"What do you think?" she countered.

"I'm sorry. I didn't mean to upset you. I promise I won't run off with the rangers … or the circus."

"Tell the rangers that I'm going to fix breakfast for them, and not to run off. And that goes for you, too."

There came a knock at the door. It was Captain Williamson. Dusty immediately invited him in.

"Am I interrupting anything?" Williamson asked.

"Not at all, Tom," Connie assured him.

"Captain Williamson, I'm about to prepare breakfast. It would be my pleasure if you and your men joined us," Jenny announced, hoping they would accept her invitation.

"No. We'll eat later. Right now we are more interested in getting a proper grave dug. Would you mind showing us the spot that Clint approved of?" Williamson requested.

"Certainly. It's wonderful that you want to do this for Clint. I know he will appreciate it greatly," Connie replied. "Come, I'll show it to you."

* * * * *

By noon, everyone, except Charlie Rhodes, had gathered at Rim Shadow Ranch. Robert had stuck close to Clint since yesterday. He was afraid of what Clint might do to himself. He was certain that his friend was feeling great guilt, and was most likely blaming himself for Lisa's death.

When Clint peered into the cedar coffin he could not believe how angelic his wife looked. The women had gone "above and beyond" to make her as lovely as possible. He was also greatly pleased at how nice the coffin looked, and conveyed his satisfaction to all those involved in its creation.

Clint reached out and touched Lisa's hand. It was not as cold as he expected it to be. He left his hand on hers briefly. Before stepping back from the coffin, he kissed her forehead. He then walked across the room and retrieved little Lena from Mrs. Myers' lap. Lastly, he walked back to the coffin, and held Lena up so she could see her mother. The little girl seemed to understand that she would not see her mother again. She leaned forward in Clint's arms and softly said: "Bye, bye."

Clint turned about and handed Lena to Connie—who was now standing next to him. He then turned to Robert, and said: "It's time."

Clint walked out onto the porch while the lid was being secured to the coffin. Dusty, Captain Williamson, Jim and Will each grabbed a rope handle and carried the coffin from the house. Robert walked with Clint, while the ladies and children followed closely behind.

Lisa was buried on a small knoll about fifty yards from the house. The graveside service was short and simple, with Robert reading an uplifting passage from his Bible. He closed the service by leading everyone in thoughtful prayer.

Following the service, Captain Williamson and his men bade farewell, and promptly departed for Fort Verde via Payson. They had a two-day journey ahead of them.

Mrs. Myers suggested that everyone gather at her home for lunch. The response was positive and unanimous.

Connie was concerned for Clint, and as such, made several attempts to comfort him. He seemed to respond somewhat to her efforts. She realized that he would need someone watching over him for a time.

Sensing that her father needed her, Lena spent a lot of time sitting in his lap, hugging him, and patting his face with her little hands.

It was nearly three o'clock when Clint expressed a desire to return home. He gathered up his daughter, thanked each and every one in the room for all their help, and departed.

Jenny decided that she should probably tag along, and hurriedly rounded up Maree and Kris. Walking quickly, they caught up with Clint and Lena.

"I think I'll tag along, too," Dusty announced.

"I thought you might, Dusty," Rebecca teased.

"Do ya think Clint will be okay?" Robert inquired of his sister.

"Clint's a strong individual. He's seen a lot of death in his lifetime. He will heal … in time. Besides, he's got a little girl to care for … and that alone will keep him focused," Connie reasoned.

Mrs. Myers sighed, then said: "I hope you're right."

"Connie, why don't you visit Clint later today. Maybe even prepare a hot meal for him and Lena," suggested Rebecca. "I know he would appreciate it."

"Jenny might take offense to that," Connie countered. "She has been doing most of the cooking for Clint and Lisa the past two years."

"Hey, Jenny will soon be cooking for *Dusty*, just in case you haven't heard the news," Rebecca disclosed, not just to Connie, but also to everyone else in the room.

"What!" Robert blurted out. "Now just when did this all come about?"

"Charlie told me yesterday," Rebecca confessed.

"Well, I'll be doggone," exclaimed Robert.

* * * * *

It was around five o'clock when Connie knocked at Clint's front door. He came to the door without delay. Lena was following him.

"Oh, Connie, please come in. What brings you by?"

"I wasn't sure if Jenny would be cooking for you tonight. And I just couldn't stand the thought of you worrying about what to fix for dinner."

"You must be a mind reader, cause I was concerned about what to fix for Lena. I'm not so hungry myself, but I know she has got to be starving."

"Where's Jenny?"

"I'm glad you asked. Somethin' strange is goin' on with that girl … and Dusty, too. She and her kids went with Dusty over to his father's place about thirty minutes ago."

"You don't say!" replied Connie, not really all that surprised by the news.

"I reckon they'll return before dark," Clint reasoned.

"Clint, are you aware that there is no one else at the house?

Charlie's in Payson … and won't be back until tomorrow. So, that could be a potential problem."

"It could? Why do you think that?" Clint asked.

"Clint, have you ever considered that they might be attracted to each other … even in love?"

"Uh, I guess it never really crossed my mind. Reckon we could pray that temptation will not overcome them; but, I trust them both to do the right thing," Clint said, with an air of assurance.

Connie reached out and grabbed Clint's upper arm and Lena's hand and escorted them into the kitchen.

"Have a seat at the table while I take a look around and see what we've got available. I use to cook at Ma Thurman's Café back in Corydon … and I was pretty darn good at it, too."

"That's comforting to know," he said with a grin.

Connie prepared a splendid meal for the three of them. For a man that claimed he wasn't very hungry, Clint put away two large helpings of food. For that, Connie was most grateful. She very much wanted him to keep his strength up. It was probably the first decent meal he had eaten since leaving home to battle the *raiders of Salt River Canyon.*

Clint helped Connie clear the table and wash the dishes. Afterwards, with little Lena in-tow, they adjourned to the front porch. They talked until it was nearly dark. Now and then, Connie detected a tear welling up in Clint's eye. She knew he was hurting—a lot.

Connie arose from her rocking chair. "Clint, I'd best be going before it gets so dark I can't see the path. I'd like to come back tomorrow to check on you and Lena. Will you need me to watch Lena while you take care of your chores?"

"I reckon Jenny can do that," Clint assumed.

"Clint, you don't know this yet, but Dusty and Jenny are getting married. Chances are, she'll be living at his place before too long."

"Married! No way! Why she's a lot older than him … and has two children as well. He wouldn't—"

"Oh, yes, he would!" interrupted Connie, smiling.

"Son of a gun! I didn't have a clue!"

"Get prepared for an empty room or two in your house. I'm guessing they will get hitched in the next few weeks. Charlie has already given them his blessing."

"How long has *he* known about this?"

"He just found out a few nights ago. Lisa brokered the whole deal. She had Charlie over for dinner so they could gang up on him. By the time it was over, Charlie was asking Lisa to find *him* a wife!"

"You're not serious? Did she have someone in mind for him?"

"Not sure. But we'll never—"

Connie stopped mid-sentence. She couldn't believe how insensitive her remark was about to become.

"Connie, it's okay. Don't feel like you have to tiptoe around me every time you have somethin' to say."

"I'm sorry, Clint. It's just—"

Clint closed the gap between them, and gave her a brief, gentle hug. "Please, Connie, don't worry 'bout me. I'll be fine. I just need some time to sort things out. I really do appreciate all you've done. I heard how you took charge of things around here yesterday and today. And I'm grateful to you."

"I just wanted to be helpful … that's all."

"And did I thank you for helping me battle those two raiders? I think not. Had you not risked your life bein' a decoy … well, there's no tellin' what they might have done to Lena. And if you don't mind me sayin' so, that was some mighty good shootin' you did."

"Thank you, Clint. When I do something … I like to give it my very best," Connie said, with a slight hint of seduction in her voice, and a gleam in her eye.

"Connie, tomorrow is Sunday, and if you'd like to stop by … well … I wouldn't mind so much."

"I'll see you around noon then," promised Connie, as she leaned forward and kissed him on the cheek. "Goodnight!"

"Goodnight, Connie!"

Clint remained on the porch with Lena and watched as Connie crossed the courtyard to intercept the path that would take her through the woods to her home. He was most grateful for her help. He considered her to be a truly caring woman.

Lena pointed at Connie and said, "Ma-ma!"

"Mama?" echoed Clint, puzzled by Lena's reaction to Connie.

"Sweetie, are you talkin' 'bout Connie?"

Lena nodded her little head, and began rubbing her red, tired eyes.

"Maybe no one told you, little one, but Connie can't be your mama. She's sweet on that preacher fella over in Payson. I think they may even be plannin' to marry someday soon."

"Ma-ma!" repeated Lena, again pointing in the direction where Connie had disappeared into the woods.

Clint scratched his head and pondered a moment about what Lena had said. He decided it was best not to try and explain things any further to her … at least for the moment.

"Come on Lena, it's time for you to go to bed."

* * * * *

Over the next several days, many of Clint's friends and neighbors stopped by to offer their condolences. Many brought prepared food. He was nearly overwhelmed by the outpouring of love, and the concern for his and Lena's welfare.

Connie, too, was concerned for Clint and Lena, and spent a lot of her free time assisting Clint around the ranch. She was amazed at how much responsibility Lisa had had when it came to helping Clint with his horses.

Connie also spent time instructing Clint on how to cook for a little girl. "Remember, Clint," she often said, "she doesn't eat steak and potatoes at every meal like some horse farmer I know!"

* * * * *

By the middle of the following week, Clint returned to Robert's ranch in order to assist him once again with the stage line duties.

Robert was glad to see his friend being active, and healing more and more each day from the tragic loss of his beloved wife.

I just don't know what I would do if I lost Rebecca, Robert thought to himself. He thanked God every day for the gift of such a wonderful helpmate, and the love she gave him.

Two weeks after Lisa's death, Sheriff Ken Hannagan paid Clint a visit. When asked why he came over on the stage, he stated that he was just too old to ride that far on a horse anymore. They had a good laugh over that. He also announced that he was retiring at the end of the year.

Not many days after Sheriff Hannagan's visit, Marshal Mike Chandler stopped by for a visit. He too came by stage—only because it was a faster way to travel. It was Chandler that first introduced Clint to Captain Williamson and his men.

And speaking of Williamson, he informed Clint, by letter, that he (Clint) would be receiving a commendation medal from the territorial governor for his outstanding service to the Arizona Rangers.

* * * * *

As the sun slowly dropped behind the distant mountains, Clint settled back into one of the front porch rocking chairs. Lena was comfortably perched in his lap.

He folded up the letter from his friend, Captain Williamson, and tucked it away in his shirt pocket. Though Clint was happy about the medal, he would trade a dozen medals just to have his *little mountain girl* back in his arms again.

Clint and Lena rocked away in the big chair as he hummed a little cowboy tune. It took only a couple of stanzas to put Lena to sleep. Clint deliberated for a moment as to how he would raise this little girl on his own.

The answer came quickly to him. He couldn't. It would take God's divine involvement to get it done. Clint took comfort in that revelation.

Epilogue

TEN MONTHS have now come and gone since the rangers battled the *raiders of Salt River Canyon.* It is now July 1895, and many changes have taken place in the *shadow of the Mogollon Rim.* Here are a few examples of those changes:

Dusty Rhodes married **Jenny Reavis** last October. Jenny and her children moved from Rim Shadow Ranch to her father-in-law's ranch. The children now refer to Charlie as Grandpa. To date, no new additions to the family are expected.

Charlie Rhodes finally met a nice woman—without any help, I might add. He met her last November, when she stepped from the stage. She had traveled to the area from Kingman. Her purpose for coming was to replace Lisa (Reavis) Wells as the new schoolteacher at Basin Flat. And, for her and Charlie's convenience, she is renting a bedroom from Mrs. Myers—Connie's *former* bedroom, that is.

Captain Williamson finally got that promotion that he had long wished for. In January, he was elevated to the grade of major, and given a job in Flagstaff as the new district supervisor. His fellow rangers, **Jim O'Bryan** and **Will Clowers**, experienced some career changes, as well. Jim was promoted to captain, and took over Williamson's position at Fort Verde; and Will resigned as a ranger, and filled the vacant sheriff's job in Show Low—at Ken Hannagan's insistence.

Mrs. Helen Myers and her niece, Connie, got that mercantile store and café built on Christopher Creek. Both businesses opened in April, and have been an overwhelming success. It is rumored that other new businesses are coming to the area. Any plans for a new schoolhouse near Christopher Creek are still on the "back burner."

Robert Lynne and his wife, **Rebecca**, are expecting their first baby sometime in August. If it's a girl, they plan to name her Lisa.

Clint Wells came to terms with the death of his wife, Lisa. Most of the credit can be given to the new woman in his life—**Connie Lynne**—or should I say, Connie Wells. They were married just last month.

So what happened to Connie's engagement to Pastor Rick Vargas, you ask? Well, it seems he fell "head-over-heels" in love with a much younger woman in his church. It was he who broke their engagement. Needless to say, he wasn't invited to the wedding. A pastor from Show Low did the honors. Most of Clint's friends showed up for the wedding—including all the rangers.

Oh, I almost forgot—Charlie Rhodes' lady friend, Abby, caught the bouquet.

THE END

About the Author

CRAIG MAIN, a United States Air Force retiree and "baby boomer," is an inspiring new author of western novels. *Raiders of Salt River Canyon* is his second novel, and the sequel to *Shadow of the Mogollon Rim.*

Though relocating recently to his home state of Indiana, he lived in Arizona for most of his adult life—beginning in January 1965. Arizona still had a significant Wild West ambiance in the early sixties, and numerous unspoiled places were always waiting to be discovered. Many ranchers still rode their horses into town on a regular basis. Western wear was the *uniform* of the day.

Craig spent a good deal of his free time camping, hiking, mountain biking, and hunting throughout central and northern Arizona, which includes the Mogollon Rim and Salt River Canyon regions. He is very familiar with the towns and locations mentioned in this exciting new novel. His character, Clint Wells, reflects his Western spirit. This is a novel that young adults and "baby boomers" alike can enjoy.